LIFE AND DEATH IN SUBURBIA

ALSO BY
ROBB SKIDMORE

The Pursuit of Cool

The Surfer

LIFE AND DEATH IN SUBURBIA

SEVEN STORIES

ROBB SKIDMORE

TMiK PRESS

LOS ANGELES

TMiK Press, Los Angeles, California

First Paperback edition

The characters and events in this book are fictitious. Any similarity to real persons, living or dead, is coincidental and not intended by the author.

Grateful acknowledgment is made to the following publications in which some of these stories were first published: *Twelve Stories:* "We Were Gods," *Oasis:* "Never Quite The Same," *The South Carolina Review:* "Space Food," *New Orleans Review:* "Hank's Place," *New Millennium Writings:* "Saunter."

ISBN: 978-0-9850379-7-0
Library of Congress Control Number: 2024915243

For Ingrid

TABLE OF CONTENTS

WHEN DADDY
CAME HOME

Gunter stood at his mailbox in a subdivision so new it was mostly dirt, the car traffic rare. He was nine and wore green Sears Toughskins jeans and a T-shirt emblazoned with the numerals '44.' A grape jelly stain, from a sandwich he'd made himself, smeared his cheek.

He straightened his spine and set his head high, per Miss Burnside's instructions regarding preparation for proper vocalization. Quick glances assured he was alone and could make attempts without scrutiny. He tilted his head up to the sun, closed his eyes and opened his mouth as if he were about to chomp on a slice of cake. His tongue darted around, producing guttural noises during the warmup. Feeling a low voltage of confidence, he jumped into his new speech therapy sentence: "The rrr....ain in Spaiin falls mmmaa..." It came apart in a series of throat spasms. He kicked the dirt, wanting to rip out his vocal chords.

A ripping, explosive sound boomed from overhead, and he watched a fighter jet tear across the sky. Was it Daddy? Was he home from Vietnam?

Approaching Mama in the evening was a tricky business. Mornings in her quilted bathrobe, before she dropped Gunter off at school and went to work as a cashier at the A & P, she was bleary-eyed and quiet. After her morning pills she perked up and liked to drive her Ford Mustang fast and play the car radio loud. "This song's a kick," she liked to say to Gunter.

But nighttime, after she'd been drinking wine, could be perilous.

"Gunter, baby," she called out from upstairs. In the kitchen he speared a clump of noodles from the pot and chewed, considering the tone of her voice: disconnected and weak, but possibly happy. Walking up the stairs, he considered that that evening she had read a romance novel and talked on the phone with her sister and had probably consumed two, but not more than three glasses of pink chardonnay. He heard a splash. She was in the tub.

In the hallway he paused, as he often did, at the official Air Force picture of his father: his crisp cap perfectly fixed on his stubbly head, his shirt so spotlessly white as to add a measure of holiness. His father looked solemn and serious, like it was a picture from a history book. He flew planes and was in a war because it was his *duty*—a word adults always said in hushed tones.

"Gunter…" Mama grew impatient.

He dug his hands into his pockets and dropped his chin as he entered her bathroom.

Mama blinked at him from the tub, smiling lazily, her head perched atop a thin layer of bubbles, her hair half-wet. "This war is almost over. President Nixon is turning it over to the Vietnamese." She added, "It's in the papers," as if Gunter hadn't believed her. "There's hope your father will be home soon." She stirred soap bubbles with her finger.

He took a step back, embarrassed by the hint of her body under the water.

"Don't be a prude." She flicked drops at him. "Did I hear that television last night?" she asked in her sly, about-to-get-mad voice.

"N…nooo." A lie. He shook his head slowly. The television, with its battle scenes from the leafy jungles of Vietnam and the footage of planes dropping bombs and North Vietnamese missile batteries that shot American planes out of the air, had been banished to the attic and covered with a blanket. Not to be watched. But when she passed out on the couch, Gunter would creep upstairs and click on the television in the dark, like it was a secret portal to another world, and watch *Gilligan's Island* or delight in the cartoon pranks that the Road Runner inflicted upon Wile E. Coyote. Last night he had witnessed an opera singer with a power and command of voice so effortless and precise it left him awestruck.

"I got another call from that principal at your school," she said matter-of-factly. Gunter tensed. Tommy Knox had followed Gunter down the hallway saying *Dumb as they come, dumb as they come.* Gunter's warning stares were met with sneers, so he punched Tommy Knox in the face, hard. Blood from Tommy's nose splattered a locker.

She took a sip of wine from a glass by the tub. "That man, what is his name… Patterson? I find him rather pushy." She glanced at Gunter, who stared at her, wide-eyed. "Now Gunter, baby. We've had that talk. Please behave." Her hand came out of the water and hung over the tub, dripping. Her red nail-polished fingers beckoned and Gunter held her warm, clammy hand.

Mama closed her eyes, like she was suddenly very tired. "We've just got to get through until Daddy gets home."

Gunter nodded.

Machine Gun Mouth, kids called him. Porky Pig had been created for his personal torture. His vocal box was a mysterious vortex. Noises and partial words might spill out like exhaust from a balky engine, or it might execute several words perfectly then jam for good. So he felt vulnerable at school. The silver lining was that he spent an hour every day, alone, with the lovely Miss Burnside.

When Gunter entered the Special Needs room, Miss Burnside, fresh out of college, always stood at attention, usually in white leggings, a short jumper dress and white turtleneck. With huge green eyes she always smiled richly then tilted her strawberry blonde braid to one side. Seeing her made Gunter feel tingly and woozy.

Mrs. Lyde, his homeroom teacher, often pointed her ruler at him accusingly, as though his vocal gymnastics were intended to provoke laughter and sow disruption. A stout, ursine woman, she smacked her hands together, trying to bring unison to his sentences like he was a lazy seal. Walking into Miss Burnside's room was like a fairy tale happy ending.

"Hello, Gunter," Miss Burnside enunciated slowly. She smiled.

'Hellllll……..ooo."

"Lose the facial tension, Gunter."

He stuck out his tongue and made a wobbly, Jell-O face.

"Good. Now let's breathe in. Wonderful."

He sucked in air until the top of his head was dizzy.

Miss Burnside pointed to Gunter's metal chair with an orange plastic seat, where he eagerly sat. She sat facing him then pointed to the white sheet that outlined Gunter's progress toward delivering his oral book report. Started weeks ago, he had read the Easy Reader George Washington biography four times, until his mind brimmed with pertinent facts such as Mount Vernon, the cherry tree and becoming the first president. His book report was written, each sentence perfected with Miss Burnside's enthusiastic help, his pencil penmanship showing a high degree of accuracy and clarity.

Now it was all about practice. Gunter stood, gripping the full text.

Miss Burnside straightened up, ready to be awed.

Gunter cleared his throat. A smile crept across his face which he failed to constrain, because Miss Burnside was already enthralled. She was eager to prove her speech therapy bona fides and possessed legendary patience. Despite the guttural car wrecks that regularly issued from his mouth, she never showed dismay.

Gunter breathed in slowly, yet fully, powering up his lungs. His lips curled back on his teeth and the first words came forth: "Georrrrge Washinnnngton was…"

Miss Burnside nodded along in bright recognition.

A week ago, he had made great progress, delivering back-to-back sentences with a passable clarity, bringing Miss Burnside to her feet clapping. He bowed, then took a victory lap around the classroom. But the next day the disfluency was back, worse than ever. He overturned his chair, fell to a pile of napping mats and pretended tears were not coming out of his eyes.

The consoling hug Miss Burnside offered was no less than transcendent.

Gunter stood before his hushed fourth grade class, his hair neatly combed. His eyes went to Mrs. Lyde who nodded that he should begin. He took a deep breath and imagined himself talking to Miss Burnside.

His first sentence about George Washington being the first president of the United States went relatively smoothly. He felt a bump of confidence. He glanced over the top of his report and found attentive classmates.

"When G… georrrrge Washingggton was a boy…"

A boy in the front row of desks bunched up his face and stuck out his tongue. Another boy snickered. Gunter gripped his report tighter with his hands. He focused intensely on the text. His breath grew short, his throat tightened.

"…chopppped chhhh…errry…errrry…"

The first boy laughed, and Gunter kicked him hard in the shin. The boy wailed loudly and Mrs. Lyde had Gunter by the arm and pulled him out of the classroom, and soon he was sitting in the lobby of Principal Patterson's office.

Gunter sat in the big smelly leather chair opposite Principal Patterson's desk, his feet dangling. His right sneaker was untied.

"So you've been at it again," Principal Patterson said, dipping his chin with displeasure. Dressed in a brown corduroy coat, his bushy eyebrows came together, his mustache quivering over his top lip.

Gunter took this in and wondered what Patterson would do. Last time Patterson had showed Gunter the large painting on the wall of Admiral Horatio Nelson's naval victory and explained that discipline and focus had won the day, and that Gunter could use some of that. Gunter had enjoyed smelling Patterson's apple scented pipe smoke and had marveled at the tall ships blasting one another with cannons while listening to Patterson's friendly, convivial tone.

"There's a place called *reform school*," Patterson said. "Boys who don't reform their behavior and who keep creating problems are sent there." Patterson scrunched up his nostrils, flashing his nose hair. He opened a file on his desk which Gunter knew to be his file. Patterson flipped papers and grimaced. "This is unacceptable."

"B...buubuut, my maaath. Mmmath sscore."

"Huh?"

Gunter gritted his teeth and fumed internally. *My math scores*, he wanted to scream. *I'm the best at math in my whole class. How about that?* But instead he pointed at the file hoping Patterson figured it out.

"Kicking, punching. There's a bite in here somewhere, Gunter. You fashion yourself a brawler. Well, at your next stop you won't win fights."

Gunter exhaled and sank into the leather chair. This would be over soon.

Apropos of nothing, Gunter decided to tie the laces of his shoe. He slid off the chair and crouched down. Patterson kept talking. Gunter noticed a black pipe lying on the brown carpet. Its ivory stem and carved wooden bowl made it seem magical and powerful, like it had fallen out of the coat of a wizard. Gunter grabbed it and put it in his back pocket. Sitting in the chair again, he tried not to squirm atop the lump.

Patterson slapped the back of his hand on the file. "Is reform school what you want? Don't just sit and stare."

"N...nooo, sirrrr."

Patterson frowned. "Not getting any better, is it? If Miss Burnside is making no progress, then maybe it's best you moved on. Or perhaps I should consider getting a better speech therapist. You're her only student. There's really no excuse."

Gunter's eyebrows went up with alarm.

Gunter sat in his chair with an orange plastic seat, going through his vocal exercises. The grunts and warbles sounded horrible even to him. His confidence was gone. His eyes kept searching Miss Burnside's face. She seemed nervous. Some darker lines creased the underside of her eyes. Days ago he had seen her coming out of Patterson's office with a stricken expression.

"Maybe we should move on today," Miss Burnside said, making a note in her new plan notebook. She glanced at his gritted teeth and said, "You're doing just fine," but her smile was quick, followed by a long inhale.

"I'm ddddoing the best… IIII'mmm…"

"I know you're doing your best, Gunter." She reached over and patted his knee. She smoothed out her skirt then gazed benevolently at him. *I won't give up*, he projected to her with his eyes. *Not ever. I'm gonna whip this shit. If no other reason than for you.*

He woke on a Saturday to knocking at the front door. He rubbed his eyes, hearing doorbell chimes. A brief silence then door knocking resumed. In Snoopy pajamas, his feet touched the cool floor. *Chutes and*

Ladders board game pieces scattered when he reached for his plaid bathrobe. Mama's door was closed. Nothing stirred inside, like it was a sealed crypt.

He opened the front door. At the street, two Air Force men in drab uniforms had just walked back to their drab vehicle. The driver, from his open door, looked back to the house. Gunter walked across the dirt yard with the vague impression one of the men might be his father. They were the same height as his father, same haircut, but one had a mustache and one had a flat nose.

"Do you live here?" one man asked, pointing at the house.

Gunter nodded. He pulled the carved pipe out of his bathrobe pocket and inhaled its apple scent.

"Is your Mama home?"

He looked back, saw her car in the driveway, and said, "Yyyyy…yes."

The man with the mustache held a leather briefcase. Gunter looked at the men with suspicion. They looked at each other, pondering what to do, then the flat nose man said, "Your Daddy has come home."

Gunter scratched his head. He looked in the backseat and did not find his father. He looked more closely at the two men. Nope. Not his father.

Gunter woke up in the deep of night. The dark outline of his Mama swayed over his bed. She reeked of liquor. That afternoon she had spoken to the Air Force men in the living room then spent the day locked in her bedroom, softly sobbing inside.

"Wake up, baby. Time to wake up," she said, in an odd, high-pitched voice. Wearing a bathrobe, her hair hung over her face and her hands pulled at his covers.

He sat up, on high alert, and wondered what time of the night it was. She took his hand and led him toward the hallway.

"Whaaaat… what's goooing on? he asked.

"Daddy has come home to us."

On the stairs she swayed into the banister. Gunter held her arm to steady her. Downstairs in the living room, candles were lit on the coffee table. They sat on the sofa. Gunter looked around the room for his father.

She grasped his hand in hers and said, "It's time to pray. Pray with me now." She pitched her head forward and back while whispering things he couldn't understand.

When she stopped Gunter said, "Wwwwhere? Wheeere… uuugg… is he?"

"His remains! They have sent his remains!" She pointed to a box wrapped in brown paper on the coffee table. "If we are to believe them, and we all know the Air Force is full of lies. But there he is." She cried softly.

Gunter pulled the box toward him—it was heavy— and read the packaging which said: *Human Remains*, along with his father's name. So that was that. His Dad had crashed or been burned up or died fighting the enemy, or something. Gunter wanted to cry but told himself not to do it.

Mama whispered and prayed again. Then she reclined into the sofa and closed her eyes. As she slept he heard the slow, barely audible rush of air from her mouth.

A crescent moon washed the backyard with gentle light. Gunter dragged a shovel to a spot near a newly planted tree. He stuck the shovel into the ground, pushed it with his full weight, then pried up fresh ground. When a modest hole was dug, he tossed the shovel aside and pressed his knees into the dirt. He looked at the box and wondered about its contents. Perhaps his Dad's disembodied hands were in there. Perhaps that was all that remained. His plan was to bury the whole box. Opening it seemed the wrong thing to do.

He placed the box in the hole. He sat back on his ankles and thought about what to say. In every Western movie there was a scene where they buried a gunfighter and then took off their hats and said kind words.

He rubbed the knees of his Toughskins jeans, moved by the importance and solemnity of the moment. He reached for the right words. All the news reports he'd seen on the attic television flashed through his mind, all the jungle reporters and sweaty soldiers and high-altitude bombers and helicopters zipping over palm trees and tumbling canisters of napalm and jets precariously landing on aircraft carrier decks. A tension crept into his stomach and jaw and brain, just as when these images had flashed before him in the dark and he had watched, half-expecting to witness his Dad being blown out of the sky by a missile, or blown up by a misplaced bomb, or any of the other scenarios Mama talked about and which rattled in his own mind as well.

They rattled no more. One of them had happened and here was the box. His body loosened and he slumped.

He cleared his throat. "Here lies my Dad," he began, so deep in his thoughts he didn't notice his voice. But had he listened, he would have found that the words were well-formed and flowed with a gentle rhythm.

WE WERE GODS

T he Creature from the Black Lagoon, Darth Vader, the Hunchback and even the Incredible Hulk at his most rage-filled and hideous had nothing on the Barger brothers. We hated and loved them. As boys verging on adolescence, we existed in elaborate swoons of fantasy, our violence both imagined and sometimes real. Can you forgive us? Should we be forgiven? We lived in a brand-new subdivision where two-story houses sprung from dirt lots. Straw and grass seed tickled our noses, competing with the tang of virgin tar which flowed down the streets. Behind our homes was a place my friends and I called the No Man's Land, and it was a paradise of no supervision. A treeless expanse of red dirt with eroded gullies and hidden canyons. Interstate power lines buzzed overhead, strung along colossal metal towers dotted with yellow and black DANGER! HIGH ELECTRICITY signs.

We were covered with Band-Aids and vibrated with hyperactive energy no dosage of Ritalin could properly contain or focus. We jumped our fancy BMX bicycles over crude ramps, crashed on the landings and flew over the handlebars, then wiped away blood and red dust from scrapes on our shins. It was a contest to destroy expensive Christmas gifts as fast as possible. We crashed remote control replica fighter planes and deliberately flew helicopters into power lines hoping to provoke power outages. We looked at dirty magazines passed down from older brothers and practiced swear words. We fired CO2 powered BB guns and arrows from compound hunting bows, exploded hundreds of dollars of Black Cats and Triple Whistlers and M-80 firecrackers. We climbed high into the metal towers and swung from crossbeams like monkeys. How did we not kill ourselves? What deity protected us from self-annihilation—the Saint of Skinned Elbows?

Hex! The diabolical Barger boys tossed them with alarming regularity. We crouched on the red dirt plateau, then took cover in a gully, the whammy spells zinging through the air like sniper bullets.

One peek at their creepy hovel was evidence enough of their depravity and poor character. Beyond the widest expanse of the No Man's Land, and down a winding path through woods, stood the faded Barger trailer on a harsh and estranged parcel of bottom land. It rested on cement blocks. Vines crept around a window screen, where a dark figure sometimes crossed. A clothesline crossed an open area trampled to packed dirt. It was difficult to stare for long without feeling eyes from the surrounding woods. The words *Barger* were painted in red letters on a mailbox by a dirt road. One Halloween, Martin got up some courage and knocked on the pitted door of the Barger trailer, standing in darkness in a Dracula costume. No one answered. He did not, as predicted, turn to stone.

The times we spied them kicking around the trailer or lurking in some corner of the No Man's Land, they never spoke, other than to grunt or make a sound like an explosion. Both the Young One and the Older One had shaved heads and sandpaper scalps. We assumed this was treatment for lice infestation, or hookworm: contracted after stepping into manure with open sores on their bare feet. They never wore shirts, just grimy cutoff jeans stained the color of their coppery skin. The one time I saw them up close, I noticed scabs on their elbows and outie belly buttons. Typically, we saw them running at a distance, flashing through the trees, jaws set, arms pumping. They went unseen for weeks, until one would emerge from the woods. Or they would pop their heads up from a gully and disappear when arrows and BBs were fired in their direction.

We spotted the Barger brothers in the Snack Lounge of the K-Mart. Seeing two baboons or werewolves would have been no less shocking. They sat in a booth in ripped tank tops, legs swinging, the blackened bottoms of their feet flashing. The Older One gnawed at the gristle remains on a corn dog stick. The Younger One tipped an onion ring box to his mouth, fried bits showering his face and tongue. They took off into the store, their dusty feet smacking the floor in an odd rhythm. We followed. They were elusive. We saw one pushing the other in a shopping cart down an Automotive department aisle. We found them in Toys ripping baseball cards out of their wrappers, stuffing their mouths with gum. They scampered away as we approached, and a plastic watch holder bounced on the floor.

Something about that empty holder enraged me. I found a Security man and breathlessly explained to him: *Theft is taking place in this store. The Bargers are stealing baseball cards and a Timex watch. They have shaved heads and live in a trailer.* He thanked me for this "valuable information," and resumed talking to an attractive cashier. The Bargers streaked across the parking lot with devious, elated faces, giggling hysterically. Their front pants pockets bulged.

Beyond being the spawn of the devil and raw savages, they were thieves. They were likely stealing things out of our backyards. Defensive measures were taken. We began day patrols, drinking from canteens, our salty sweat mixing with cool water. Holes were dug on a perimeter near our back yard fences, then covered with plywood and handfuls of dirt, forming a booby trap Maginot Line. We swore to capture and interrogate the Bargers. Interrogation wasn't my idea. I didn't know what that meant, but I was going with it. I mean, we were just kids, right?

We spotted them swinging from a knotted rope. We plunged into the woods on bikes to flush them out. They ran out into sunshine, heading for an electrical tower. Fleeing seemed to confirm their guilt, their evil nature, and a viciousness crept into our bodies. That can be quite a high. We fired bottle rockets that snapped over their heads. They jumped into a ditch, the Older One's head bobbing even with the ground as they ran. We headed them off at the far end and threw rapid-fire dirt clods.

On open ground, we had them in a crossfire. I sailed arrows past their heads. Was I trying to hit them? I guess I was. One arrow sliced a calf and the Older One cried out in pain. We couldn't pump our guns fast enough. BBs smacked against their legs and backs. We grabbed the Younger One and pinned him long enough for several hard punches, bloodied his nose and kicked him in the balls before he got away limping. He sobbed twice, in a pitiful kid way. It snapped me out, but not long.

Then they were gone forever. Gone from the No Man's Land, gone from their trailer. We celebrated but to be truthful, we were rather sad.

Older kids kicked out the trailer's windows and littered beer cans inside, a desecration we somewhat resented, since we didn't do it ourselves. I'm not sure who lit the match. Probably Martin, the pyro. In any event, the trailer caught fire easily and roared to life with tall orange flames and pumping black smoke. We cheered as the sides caved in. The power and terror of it ripped at our chests. We were gods. The Bargers could never return. We had achieved final victory.

It sounds odd to report these things to you, but I am merely reporting our state of mind as precisely as possible. And the accuracy of our state of mind then or at any time is, of course, highly suspect and prone to improbable notions.

LIFE AND DEATH
IN SUBURBIA

A white van made its way—an anonymous cube, a ghost of the roadway. Geoff drove with fingers tight on the wheel, engine vibrations traveling to the pit of his stomach. When driving it was hard to not think about what he was doing. Red Mike beside him, boxes of speakers slid around in back. Their bloodstreams thick with Red Bull and high test ganja, their eyes loped side to side to a hip hop pulse.

They swooped into a parking lot toward a twentyish male in a tie and sunglasses. "Speakers! Whoa, we got speakers!" Red Mike yelled in a game show voice, and the van screeched sideways into a handicapped spot.

The sliding door opened with a sheer, eviscerating sound and they jumped out like super heroes. *We just made our last delivery for Stereo City. They gave us an extra pair of speakers! They're not listed in the delivery manifest!* Geoff flipped through papers, shaking his head. Red Mike did an energetic monkey dance and Geoff high-fived him. *We just want to get rid of them. In ten minutes we have to get back to the store!*

The young man struggled to understand. Red Mike caressed the boxes, musing aloud: *Top of the line, Swiss made, diamond-balanced, the most outrageously advanced speakers to emit sounds of clarity and godlike perfection and make audiophiles cry tears of appreciation. Worth twelve hundred bucks retail! Just read the specs*, which Geoff thrust forth, conveniently laminated. The young man's body language eased. The system had coughed in his favor. *We'll take, I don't know, three hundred? Sure, two fifty will do!*

Geoff and Red Mike plopped down two boxes and roared off with fresh cash, almost convinced themselves the speakers were more than a slapdash box containing three dollars' worth of wire and solder, assembled by squatting Bangladeshi workers, with the sound quality of an ailing transistor radio. Red Mike lit a cigarette, muttering their close was weak. Geoff watched the side mirror for cops—the upper mirror, not the lower bubble where, should his gaze stray, his likeness always stared him in the eye.

Geoff grew up in a tract house indistinguishable from sixty other vinyl-sided boxes. As if a giant hand had sheared clean the land, then spilled houses from the sky. He was long and gangly, wide-shouldered with a hovering walk. A lawn was actually an ecosystem, he thought. He chanted scientific names of insects—*cordillacris occipitalis, metador pardalinus*—as his eyes scanned the grass. He pinched a grasshopper for close inspection, flicking away the naughty *orthoptera* with a finger when it spurred him. Frogs, squirrels and moles scurried out from a remaining cluster of woods, to be flattened by cars. He did dis-sections with a pocketknife, a rich scent of decay in his nostrils, working stoically, as he imagined the park rangers did in distant, wilder places.

Mom lived in Maine, a distant wild place, with her post-divorce family. Dad worked for a telecom company, wearing an orange hat and threading spools of fiber optic cable into buried PVC pipe. A burly, self-deprecating man. The stock price of the telecom shot into orbit. Having toiled there most of his life, Dad's 401(k) climbed into the high six figures, eclipsing generations who had aspired to nothing more than repairing machines or county work. "Now see," Dad said, proudly showing Geoff a statement, "this is how hard work pays off." A fishing boat of sparkling purple lacquer graced their driveway. Then the stock collapsed, and amid a flurry of insider trading and accounting irregularities, the telecom went bankrupt.

Unemployed and broke, Dad sunk to the couch, unable to rise. Geoff tried to cheer him up. He reenacted Three Stooges routines and flapped his arms like a swooping pterodactyl. Then he noticed a dark spot the size of a dime on the back of Dad's neck. A surgeon left behind a crater riven with stitches. Aggressive chemo, though unproved against this Stage III cancer, was begun. They sold the fishing boat. Their best (and perhaps only) hope, doctors said, was a newly approved drug, Hextroll, which cost $5,000 a month. Their HMO refused to cover it. Dad moved from the couch to his bedroom. He seemed to calculate that instead of wasting money they didn't have, he would grit his teeth and let the mutant cells consume him from within.

Geoff noticed a penetrating silence in the house, disturbed only by *pows* and crashes from his video games, by magnification change ticks of his microscope. The letter slot creaked and fresh mail dumped onto a growing mountain. He gathered the unpaid bills. Eighteen, he was the only one in the house standing on a regular basis.

A warehouse beside rail tracks and surrounded by barbed wire did not seem, as the ad promised, a place to earn REAL MONEY, REAL FAST. A ponytailed man in a leather vest, the boss, asked if Geoff could sell speakers. Geoff asked what kind of speakers and who were the customers and where was the showroom? The boss flashed a fake, displeased smile, then turned his back to answer his cell. Geoff sensed he'd screwed up. Finally the boss said Geoff was on one week probation and pointed to a white van.

Geoff climbed in and shut the door. A stout, freckled guy with thick red dreadlocks like a tangled mop sat behind the wheel, smoking. Red Mike flicked cinders onto his cargo pants. "Gallardo is my partner. I'm not moving without him."

"I was assigned to this van. I'm Geoff."

"*Geoff,*" he said mockingly. He had a wide face and

fleshy arms dotted with tattoos.

"Maybe I'll be better than Gallardo. Probably I will."

"Nope, you won't."

"How are you so sure?"

"Cause I'm looking at you." He slammed the door and marched over to the boss. They yelled at each other, the boss yelling louder. Red Mike got back into the van, jerked into reverse and drove away, his middle finger dancing in the boss's direction. Geoff burst into a stuttering laugh Red Mike didn't seem to appreciate.

Red Mike's black t-shirt said: Anarchist Soccer Collective, Local 24. They drove past a super-sized discount chain Geoff had first worked at when he reluctantly quit high school. He'd worn a blue vest and tried to console himself that it was *only temporary, just temporary* as he shelved detergent bottles, then realized he could clone himself into four vests and still only afford ten days a month of Hextroll.

Red Mike scowled and said, "I wish I could firebomb that place." He seethed about overseas child labor and predatory pricing that put mom and pop stores out of business.

"I worked there two weeks," Geoff said. "Didn't pay much."

"Good thing you quit. A slave no more. Here's to freedom."

Red Mike was fond of running red lights, changing lanes at high speed and running his mouth about corporate globalization. His eyes darted comically behind ugly black frame glasses. Geoff tried to get his mind around why the World Bank was trashing Third World cultures and enslaving them with debt, and what they were doing with these speakers.

Red Mike bellowed to a group of braces-wearing teenagers, "Speakers! Oh, my God! You have to see these speakers!" Then from the side of his mouth to Geoff, "*Enthusiasm, please*," and Geoff yelled, "Hey, speakers!" but the teens were already at Mike's window. Red Mike told an improbable story about delivering speakers and suddenly he and Mike were the oldest of pals. Two teens used ATM cards to get cash. As Geoff and Red Mike sped away, Geoff noticed identical boxes in the back. A hollow feeling opened in the bottom of his lungs, a trap door swinging open.

"How do you feel," Geoff asked, "about, you know… what you're doing?"

"You mean what *we're* doing. They want speakers, they get speakers. Caveat emptor. The price is freely negotiated." Red Mike gestured for the car ahead to move, then punched the horn. "Consumer craving is a powerful force. Think of the billions spent on advertising every year. The money has to go somewhere. Those hundreds could go to some crappy chain store in the mall or they can go to you and me."

Geoff rolled down his window, unconvinced, but impressed by this well-reasoned defense. The cash fanned out in Geoff's fingers, thick and papery, and he reflected on the exhilarating, if creepy nature of this transaction. But wasn't Pasteur's discovery of yeast fungus, like many scientific discoveries, essentially an accidental thing, an unexpected find? Red Mike stomped the brake at the last moment for a red light. Feeling growing nausea, Geoff asked to drive.

"Okay, man," Red Mike said doubtfully, "Let's see how you do."

Geoff circled a mall parking lot until a blonde girl in low-rise jeans clutching designer shopping bags stepped off a sidewalk. Rolling beside her, Geoff gave her the pitch. Red Mike whispered pointers: *Don't go there. Keep smiling. Go for the close.* She kept walking, listening faintly, stopping only to kick a pebble out of her sandal. *Unbelievable*, Red Mike muttered. Finally she pointed her thin, sharp nose at Geoff and said, "How do I know you really work there?" A shrewd, knowing smile formed on her lips.

"Paperwork." Geoff held up papers and smiled. Never before had such a girl paid this much attention to him.

Celeste, her silver necklace said. She inspected the glossy boxes closely, "At least you're not shitting me about these speakers. They're expensive. My brother's into sound systems. How much?"

Geoff opened his mouth and Red Mike cut in, "It's seventy percent off, but we'll take five hundred."

Geoff discreetly kicked Red Mike.

"No way." She swung a key chain, her eyes fixed, calculating. "Four hundred."

"Deal."

Her eyes darted around to see if anyone was watching, then went joyously big. She rocked on her toes and said, "So, how are these street deals concluded, boys?" They went to an ATM, then fit the boxes into her convertible BMW. She directed them, fretting about scratches on her leather. She winked and drove off.

"Five hundred?" Geoff said. "That's insane."

"Damn right. That rich little bitch"—Geoff disliked this description—"made our day. It's produce or perish. The boxes cost us five bucks a pair and the boss man gets twenty percent of the profit."

A satisfying wad of cash grew inside Geoff's jeans. In a month, he held the first bottle of Hextroll up to his eyes. He put great faith into each capsule: the yellow and gray speckled granules, the tiny white numbers, the sulfur smell. Each cost a hundred sixty-nine dollars, so he imagined each to have an awesome healing power— the fruit of the finest scientific minds, of thousands of research hours in spotless laboratories.

Geoff put the bottle beside Dad, who lay naked on his bed. The lymph node surgery and chemo had shed a coat of fat to reveal a sinewy, smaller man. Head shaved, he rarely wore clothes, like an ascetic monk. "All this cannot affect your future," he said. "We'll be home schooling from here to college." Finally, he looked at the Hextroll, slowly shaking the bottle. "Where is it you're working?"

"A warehouse." It was partly true, but equally a lie.

"A *warehouse*. Making this much money?" A fearsome light burned in his eye, last seen when as an umpire he ejected an enraged father from a softball game, sending the man away cowed and quiet. Then Dad shut his eyes in disgust, and held them tight, as if inwardly focusing this emotion. He let out an exhausted breath.

"Does it matter where?" Geoff said, as his father fumbled with a painkiller bottle.

Geoff found Advanced Biology, Modern Forestry and Chemistry textbooks on his desk, topped by a lesson plan. He turned pages, smudging them. His hands stank with an oily van smell, grime under his fingernails. He had thought of the future as birthdays and rosy things you looked forward to, but it was different: the future was bound up in the present, and was struggling to break free.

The sprawling sunbelt city—with its metro center, gentrifying neighborhoods and suburbs thickening with retail and office centers, spreading into exurbs—proved to be ripe hunting grounds. Around every corner were college students, yuppies, and professionals. All hungry for high end sound. An ecosystem became apparent: it meant nothing to plunk down several hundred bucks when they were going anyway, like a green-lighted car sprinting away from a white line. There were five cell phone distributors and dry cleaners per square mile, as though people would drop if money stayed in their pockets too long.

Geoff and Red Mike traveled the common roadways. Quick marts and 7-Elevens fulfilled their immediate needs. They shuffled past roofers and delivery people, nameless fixers and painters, their white van comrades, to use toilets crawling with mold, to buy revolving hot dogs and sugary mega drinks. They ebbed and flowed in traffic, the monotony punctuated by the occasional terror of avoiding mangled plastic on the roads. They circulated in the highway system in much the way killer T-cells and cytotoxic drugs combatted cancer cells in a body, the mutant cells under attack in the battle for lymph nodes. And Hextroll led the fight!—whacking cancer cells, sucking them dry. It was undeniable: the scientists had witnessed this under their powerful electron microscopes.

Geoff's first tattoo, a dragon on his left forearm, came on a dare from Red Mike. He imagined the queasy stab of the needle to be what his father felt in chemo. He loved the flex of his veins and muscles underneath the red and blue dragon, the way strange eyes were drawn to it. *See me and beware*, it announced. More tattoos followed. He challenged himself with how many hours he could take the pain.

Downtown, a trash-laden breeze whipped through a high-rise corridor. "Speakers. Hey guys, check it out," Geoff said to a trio of suit wearers. They smirked but failed to break stride, and also ignored a raving homeless man. Red Mike said, "Stupid assholes," and tossed pebbles, bouncing them at their polished heels.

"The hatred," Geoff said. "Let up on the hatred, man."

"Think those guys would accept you or me? Think they would let us join their golf club?"

"Once I go to college they might," Geoff said. But the rare nights he opened his textbooks, his eyes fell shut from exhaustion. *Mitochondria* seemed a ludicrous abstraction.

"Oh, yeah. Joe College. You still don't get it." Red Mike had gone through a series of juvenile arrests and drug misadventures, before his father, a wealthy entrepreneur, evicted him down the front steps of his home with the backside of his hand. When Red Mike wasn't listening to revolutionary speed metal, he was designing computer viruses or directing his piss at shiny tassel loafers at the urinal beside him.

Red Mike picked up a brown lump in the gutter—a wallet. "Yes! Papa needs a new Play Station!" He sniffed a shiny credit card. Geoff snatched both away. Red Mike complained all the way to the post office, where Geoff addressed a bubble envelope and mailed the wallet to its owner. Red Mike poked Geoff in the chest and said, "Think you're *Joan of fucking Arc*? Think again."

A white sun-bleached ledge outside the mall, on a day off. A blonde girl locked eyes with Geoff. Then something stung his shoulder, knocking him off the ledge. A purse—leather, buckled and heavy—had banged against him. A silver necklace danced at the girl's throat: *Celeste.* "How could you do that to me?" she said. "You are so evil! I want my money back!"

"Stop. Okay," he said, hands raised in surrender. "I'll give your money back. I'm sorry." Two older women stared from the sidewalk. A mall security truck crossed the lot, yellow light flashing. He dug through his pockets and found fifty dollars. A feeling he'd long dodged now consumed him like a warm bath: he was a leech, a creep, a criminal.

She shoved the money into her jeans, calmly and in control. "Is that all you got? Where's the rest?"

"Let's go inside to an ATM," he said, guiding her towards a department store. She answered her chirping cell purposefully as she walked, sucked into a conversation with a girlfriend. She stopped at a rack of jeans and hummed with interest. She examined jeans and chatted for a minute, her eyes subtly wandering to study Geoff. She said, "Meet me back here. Do you swear?"

"Sure," he said, baffled by her.

"I could still call security," she said, suppressing a smile, her eyes wide in a mischievous, possibly joking way. She turned her back quickly, resuming her conversation. In the atrium he knew he had ditched her, but running would have made her opinion true. The tight cling of her T-shirt also crossed his mind. His account had two hundred bucks. He withdrew eighty. It took a while to find her in the department store. She clicked through a rack of blouses, sailing gauzy fabrics through the air, scrutinizing workmanship, reading labels, making appraisals of style and color, and flipping winners to a waiting sales assistant.

Geoff waved the cash, but failed to get her attention. "I'll have to owe you."

Finally she took the cash, in the same motion putting an expensive designer men's dress shirt against his chest. "This would look so awesome on you."

"I can't afford that," he said, looking at the tag.

"At least try it on."

Inside the dressing room, she stood behind him, cool and serious. His t-shirt fell to the floor. The bright scientific light made each tattoo active, lurid. On his arms a dragon snarled at a turquoise sea serpent, and a green samurai warrior challenged a Viking queen, and on his chest a Burlington Northern locomotive barreled across a high trestle. Surprised by his transformation, he gazed with a sense of alienation at the freaky clash of symbols, at the stubble on his tanned head and his newly chiseled jaw. Celeste's eyes did a dance along his limbs and she tilted her head dreamily. Hands on his waist, he tensed his biceps. Suddenly he was the outlaw, the bad boy, with a princely armor of ink. He pulled on the subtle patterned shirt, its fine cotton smooth against his skin. She flattened and arranged his collar, her eyes rising to his. She stepped back, studying the shirt. "It looks hot on you."

"I like it," he said. "Can't afford it."

"My treat then. Keep it on." She used a Visa. Wearing his new shirt, it seemed only natural to jump into her convertible, sun warming their young faces. She smiled, telling him that the speakers had worked five scratchy minutes before fatal malfunction. Her brother told her father and her ATM card, though thankfully no credit cards, was confiscated for three weeks. A time of horrible deprivation.

"Selling speakers on the street, must be kinda dangerous." She stuck out her chin and her eyes twinkled again.

He rolled up his sleeves and smiled, indulging her. "Let's just say we stay on the move…" During evenings he and Red Mike had been opening the van's door and hinting to inebriated clubgoers that their "source" had scored an electronics shipment, now at deep discount. This hint at darker illegality made people swarm. He told Celeste about the short Russian guy who had demanded a cut; Geoff shoved him into a wall. Later, they learned the Russian was an actual mobster. He laughed, reliving the sweet high of that shove—problem met, problem solved. She echoed his laugh.

"You must make *lots* of money."

"We do pretty good."

"Why can't you afford a new shirt after ripping off people all day?"

He winced at *ripping off*. "It's a temporary thing. In a few years I'll be in college."

"And study what?"

"Biology. I want to work for the Park Service, in National Parks."

She started to laugh, but stopped when she saw his face. She became sulky, as if she pictured a fat middle-aged guy in the green jacket. She smiled. "I think you're telling me stories again."

"Actually I'm not." He raised his eyebrows to prove his sincerity.

"I'll show you where I live." She drove into a wealthy suburb, past opulent houses. They went up a long driveway of meticulously uniform bricks, to a sprawling French Provincial in cream stucco with a three-car garage. A pool glowed in the back.

"Are we going inside?" he asked, excited by the prospect. She flashed a flirty expression, and nudged her chin toward him. He moved his face closer, then she pressed soft, warm lips against his. Her eyes swiveled toward the windshield, then she squinted into an open garage slot. It was dark inside, almost dark enough to conceal its contents, but a ghostlike bumper gave it away: a big black sedan. "Oh, my God! George is home!"

"George?" he said, dazed from the kiss.

"It's my *Dad*," she said with annoyance. She took a full breath and removed her hands from the steering wheel. "You might want to roll your sleeves down," she said, frowning.

"Maybe I should take off," he said resentfully.

She casually checked her face in the mirror. "You still owe me money. So behave yourself." He followed her, rolling down his sleeves. A side door led into a kitchen worthy of a magazine, a glittering place of stainless steel and veined olive marble, with lighting so subtle and varied it was enchanting. His thought had been to wait it out, to blend in with doorways as the sullen young man and hopefully be left alone. But seeing the grandeur, he wanted to assert himself.

Celeste rushed to a man in a tie and gray trousers, hugging him. Dad's face glowed with a generous delight. He asked, "What did you buy today for me?" and they both chuckled. She introduced Geoff as a "friend," and Dad stared flatly. An Asian woman in a white smock folded a towel next to the sink. She slid unobtrusively from the kitchen. Dad had dark slicked-back hair. He was well-preserved for his age, trim, with lean, taut muscles under his dress shirt. Standing perfectly erect, his eyes focused with scrutiny.

Geoff extended his hand. His sleeve retracted a few inches at the wrist, revealing a red tendril of tattoo. Dad grasped his hand. He turned the wrist upward, noting the tattoo, then released. "It's nice to meet you Geoff."

Celeste had deserted the room. A recessed light cast a warm column onto Geoff's head. Dad asked where Geoff was attending school.

"Actually I'm not in school right now."

"So you've already gone to college?"

"Not yet. I'm working."

"And what is that?"

"I'm in sales. Stereo equipment."

Dad's eyes trailed to the floor as if he had lost all interest.

"And you, sir. What do you do?"

Using minimal effort to speak, he said, "I operate two hedge funds." He picked up a bottle of Korean ginseng capsules. A long diatribe of Red Mike's came to mind, that hedge funds were the latest unregulated wave of high-risk capitalism. Only the super wealthy could afford them and according to Red Mike, they would hold the financial system hostage when bailed out by the feds.

"Trading is wide open with a hedge fund, right?" Geoff said. "And you've invested much of your own money."

Dad placed a capsule gingerly between his lips and picked up a glass of water. "That's right. Very good, Geoff."

"And you get a percentage of the profit."

"*If* there's a profit. And I've had one nine out of ten years."

Geoff suddenly felt great admiration for this man, for the wits and gumption that had led him to the top of his heap, to this showplace kitchen. He wanted to invest a huge sum of money with him.

Dad strolled around the island then turned, his eyes targeting Geoff in a searching way. "Stereo equipment, huh? I wish Celeste had known you before. She was the victim of scam artists. Four hundred bucks—isn't that awful! But I know people. I've been on the phone with the FBI. I know where these criminals are operating from. A warehouse. I'm going to nail their balls to the wall."

Geoff struggled to breathe. It seemed conceivable FBI agents might appear from every direction.

"Have you heard of these people?"

"No, sir. Well…yes, from her."

Dad stood staring at his shoes, looking older, suddenly melancholy. "I don't know how people could stoop so low."

Dad's cell phone chimed. He answered the way his daughter did: alert, but carefully judging whoever wanted to curry his favor. Geoff fled the room. A carpeted stairway led down to a connected suite of rooms bathed in lavender. Celeste sat on a day bed, knees pulled to her chest, her face fixed with rage. A growling terrier patrolled the floor before her. In a scolding whisper, she said, "You should have said *nothing*." She rolled her eyes. "Stereo salesman?"

"I have a right to talk."

"Not if you're a…."

The dog jumped and nipped his hand, drawing blood.

"Are you okay?" she asked. She fretted at the wounded hand. "You need to leave. Just get out." She moved him toward a glass outside door. Suddenly, he was standing in a side yard. The lock clicked on the door. Inside, Celeste turned her back. Pain shot through his hand.

He jumped over a decorative fence and landed on a blooming lily. He stomped several stalks, relishing the destruction. He felled a row of zinnias soccer-style, exploding the petals, then pushed over a birdbath which busted a colorful ceramic gnome. He regained the path and strolled past the Asian woman, who stood on a landing with a cat. She looked at him with disgust.

Walking down the front drive, every dovetailed brick seemed a rebuke, a taunt. Dad stared from the top of the lawn, clutching a cordless phone and holding out his free arm like a gunslinger. There were no sidewalks and traffic was fast. Geoff was forced to walk across the bottoms of lawns. Eyes in windows noted the trespasser. Two police cruisers sped down the street past him, blue lights flashing. He broke into a run.

He felt a record sense of impatience sitting with his Dad in the specialist's examination room. He *tap tap tapped* on the wall with a tongue depressor, blinking rapidly, trying to remember his Dad's last red blood cell count. Red Mike had scored this crystal powder. It gave them a magical enthusiasm for hawking speakers, and limitless energy to their pitches. It made the whole enterprise abstract and without consequence—a real life video game where you battled the clock to collect cash. The only problem: no sleep.

From the table, Dad said, "What's wrong with you?"

"Too much sleep. Not enough coffee. I mean, you know…"

Dad shifted on the crinkly sheet, a weird yellow pallor glowing inside him. His bones protruded from every angle. A hard push would have broken him.

The doctor entered the room. His eyes were already in retreat, glued to the safety of the file in his hands, and Geoff knew. He announced that tests had confirmed in-transit metastases had spread to secondary lymph nodes. Geoff snapped the depressor, the halves clicking on the floor.

The doctor asked him to please pick that up. "Stop taking the Hextroll immediately. And the remaining pills should be flushed." He explained that its manufacturer had fudged their clinical trials, overstating Hextroll's effectiveness and failing to report liver toxicity as a serious side effect. The doctor puffed his cheeks and made slow head shakes. "It boils down to a breach of trust." A silence followed, punctured by a stool squeak like the tiniest of screams.

Geoff waited for an apology, for the silver lining, for yelled threats.

In an absent voice, Dad said, "Well, Christ…" then seemed to forget the matter.

"So," the doctor said, with a manufactured gusto, "Let's see how we're doing today."

Geoff left the room and walked around the building several times, gaining speed with each turn. That night, standing over the toilet, he poured the last seven Hextrolls into his hand. The tiny white numbers caught his eye. He crammed them into his mouth and gulped them down with tap water.

At 3:00 a.m. the empty Dunkin Donuts shone in the night. Geoff's heart raced, a hopelessly up-tempo DJ at the controls. This Japanese doctor, an immune-herb genius, had a clinic in Austria, and internet testimonials from advanced melanoma patients who doctors had given up on. Total recovery. Four weeks of treatment was fifty grand, upfront. Red Mike agreed, the speaker gig wouldn't last much longer. Two guys in an unmarked car were permanently parked across the street from the warehouse. A local investigative reporter had been dogging crews with a hidden camera.

"Fifty grand. How am I going to get fifty grand?" Geoff wondered aloud. His eyes slid closed, and he jerked awake.

Red Mike stuffed half a cruller into his mouth. "Where the hell did you get fifty grand?" His hand trembled, spilling coffee as it neared his lips.

"No. It's fifty grand I need. To go to Austria."

"Right. Korean doctor. Herbs are powerful." He slapped shut his laptop. "Oh man, listen to this. My friend drives an armored car. He was telling me this one route has only one guy to pick up money from banks. It's like two hundred grand in the truck. What a scam *that* would be."

Geoff felt his dry, scaly lips. "That's not a scam, that's a felony."

"Sometimes," Red Mike lapped at an imaginary ice cream cone, "it's four hundred in the truck."

Geoff was dubious about this supposed friend. Red Mike always had a friend who nearly died from bee stings, who had met Paul McCartney in a taxi, who dressed frequently as a Klingon, etc. Geoff found a fresh coffee stain on his shirt—Celeste's shirt, as he still considered it. He noticed food stains on a sleeve, a cuff unraveling, a dull coat of grime. Once beautiful, after a month of continuous wear he had ruined it.

Suddenly Dunkin Donuts was filled with drunk teenagers. They shouted, ran back and forth to the bathroom, and threw donuts. They laughed in high-pitched voices, calling each other nicknames. Had Geoff ever been like them? He glared with resentment, his shirt growing taut over his chest. A girl whined about studying for midterms and Geoff's rage peaked. *Look at me. Just look at me.* Suddenly aware of him and Red Mike, they whispered among themselves and then left.

A tepid dawn light filled the lot. They drove away in the van, empty of boxes, but filled with hope. The working class hope of filling it with more stuff, of motoring down the road somewhere new. They parked in front of a bank ATM. Had it ever been so quiet? They stared, unmoving, like they were in church. Red Mike talked about Austria and their historic ties to Hungary and the ancient empire they once forged. The crystal was wearing off. Geoff was so tired he was alert again, in a ghostly, scoured clean way. More connected to reason than ever. Austria was a fairy tale, a gelatin capsule of dreams, and there was no need to go. A welling rushed toward his eyes, then he felt nothing.

Within this lull, an armored car pulled up to the bank, and a single rotund man got out. He walked with a limp, forever delayed in his schedule by a short leg. It seemed only natural, in the way of gain and loss, of the chaotic turning of the universe and all its lurching ecosystems and reversals and the general way things went down, that Geoff would produce a revolver, stashed long ago under his seat for an unknown eventuality, and Red Mike would produce a pistol from his messenger bag, and the limping man would exit the bank with bags of money.

NEVER
QUITE THE SAME

Diana, the leasing agent here at Windham Gate, who I mistakenly assumed to be my friend, phones me and says, "Mr. Grund, it is now the end of the month. We do not have your rent, *once again*. A remainder is due. You signed a lease."

I struggle to fake friendliness when I say: "Diana, I explained to you before that I haven't been able to pay because I haven't been paid for my last assignment." It's a hazard of being a freelance artist. Before you look down your nose, know I am an art school graduate, one of the semi-prestigious ones.

"It's a contract you signed," she says in a firm, yet sing song voice.

"Hey, I will honor my contract. They told me they've sent the check." Which is true. I illustrated a children's book—flat fee, no royalty—for a publisher in Chicago and mailed it last week. Typical children's story: a bear named Arthur gets lost in the woods when he doesn't listen to his parents. Other animals befriend Arthur, help him find his way and teach him lessons like paying attention to his surroundings and listening to his parents who set rules because they love him.

It's a beautiful world these kids live in.

I got sucked into freelance. There's this pay rent to survive thing. I don't want to say it's a trap. I have no delusions I'm the next Julian Schnabel or Jeff Koons, but I *will* say I'm working on an oil series. My blend of abstract expressionism delves heavily into Picasso's cubist phase and French pointillism, and uses the color orange in vivid and unique ways. A visiting art school lecturer, a man with L.A. ties who obviously had refined taste, was moved to say they were "remarkable."

I hang up, the cradled cordless phone still pulsating with the tension of my conversation with Diana and all its unpleasantness. She gave no guarantees. Such is life immediately before the new millennium.

When I first met her, she told me it was a community I would be moving into, not just a regular apartment complex. We rode around Windham Gate in a golf cart, wind streaming through her hair. The model suite was decked out in chrome designer furniture, like James Bond lived there. Being at Windham was like having a big family, she said. Everyone had activities together: cookouts, pool parties or just plain hanging out. Most had jobs in the city and wanted a nice place with quiet. She sent me a signed birthday card after I moved in.

I sit at my drafting table. I am working on a children's book of my own. One strategy is to write and illustrate my own children's book, sell it, keep the royalties, profit handsomely. I have no idea about the likelihood of these events. There is no storyline to the book yet, just pictures I have drawn of llamas, pythons and some creatures with antennae and dragon tails that look like space aliens. What these creatures are doing together I do not know.

I've liked living in my six hundred fifty square foot one bedroom here at Windham Gate. It's nice to have two rooms: the walk into the living room from the bedroom is like being transported to another place. I am then surrounded by different things: like my four Van Gogh prints, all painted in the period when he lived in the Yellow House in Arles, France. He painted fields, churches, peasant women—his best paintings, in my opinion. He had not yet gone completely bonkers and cut off his ear. Arles was a good place for him.

Now there's this money problem, but they are being relatively decent. At another place I lived, after the five-day grace period they placed an orange PRELIMINARY EVICTION! notice on the door handle which brands you with a scarlet letter of ineptitude or financial impotence, depending on your situation. Before that happens here, I should get my money from Chicago for *Arthur in the Aspens*. Presumably, Arthur is lost somewhere in the Rocky Mountains, though I don't know how a bear could get lost in the woods. Of course, the premise of every children's book is that the main character, whether animal, vegetable or mineral, has the same problems of a normal human kid.

I walk the apartment complex at night. Not a soul is out, the shades are all drawn, the cars all parked. They are resting before their next commute and another day of toil in the city. People keep to themselves, except for whoever was stealing my morning paper months ago. I am almost certain it was the Camaro Guy that lived on the second floor. It started the week he moved in. When my Saturday or Sunday paper was missing, I strained to listen at his door and always heard a television, but could never detect any rustle of newsprint. The guy moved out. I never saw a moving truck—he just vanished in the night. No more Camaro in the parking lot, no more missing papers.

The pool is placid under moonlight, and I stroll past buildings one through five. A lovely maple shades the space between four and five. One of the few indigenous trees left around here. The others are starter trees, sprouting out of piles of wood chips and discarded soda cans.

The 7-Eleven at the end of the street beckons with a dim glow. I think of the unspoken dread that hung about art school: the idea that real excellence in art only comes with suffering. That the reason Edvard Munch could pour out *The Scream* and other ground-breaking Northern Expressionist paintings is that he sucked into his veins lots of sanatorium visits, empty cupboards and filth. Maybe my walks to the 7-Eleven, past derelict curb sitters, to buy beefy jerky or glance at the magazine rack, have stoked some future payoff.

Back at my building, I say hello to the older divorced woman who lives on the ground floor. She is pulling her coat out of her car. She regards me warily before scurrying to her door to lock herself in with a *thunk*. The day she moved in she introduced herself, said she'd just got a divorce, that husband got the house.

"If you need anything, just knock on my door," I said.

She never has. I knocked on hers once, to ask if they were raising her rent too.

"Not to my knowledge," she said, without fully opening her door or unlatching the chain. When our cars pull into the parking lot at the same time she lingers, gathering something on the seat or fiddling with the glove compartment. I am walking up the stairs by the time she opens her car door. I live less than thirty feet from a person determined to negate my humanity.

Windham Gate has been better than my last place at Tarry Hall apartments, which looks okay when you drive by. The leasing center looks like an English Tudor mansion and inside there are flowers, balloons and soft cushions—the leasing agents look and smell like contestants in the Miss America pageant, and the building with a vacancy in it they point to looks like a cozy Welsh country cottage.

Then, on move-in day, you carry your lamp up the stairs and open the door and it's Dicken's London: a yellowing toilet, rusting metal shelves in the medicine cabinet, a hasty all-white paint job (over nails and wall hangers), a musty smell that lingers in the air and dust in the cracks of the kitchen that no amount of cleaning can remove. You take a deep breath because you have signed a contract. You tramp down the stairs, over the dirt to the U-Haul. They don't have any pretense of planting grass, it's bare soil. If you want grass you pay $300 a month more for the same space at The Presidential—a luxury community, where they have manicured lawns and tulips and a Zen garden and a pass key workout room and two pools. But you couldn't afford that, so you move everything through the doorway past the security peep-hole, turn on some music, sit in the clutter and try to relax, and imagine how the year will go and hope that it will go well. One year. More if you renew.

The one good thing about Tarry Hall was that I met Linda. She moved into the apartment across from mine. Some of her stuff sat in the back of a truck: an antique blue couch worthy of *Gone With The Wind*, a print of Edward Hopper's *Nighthawks* and hand-made birdhouses of recycled wood and plastic—her hobby. She seemed an interesting sort and I offered to help her move in.

"Thanks, I could use it," Linda said, wearing runner's clothes, exhausted, but radiant. Dark bangs lay sweat-plastered to her forehead.

"Move-ins are hell," I said.

Linda had moved out of her old place days before—ex-boyfriend troubles—and had been holed up in a motel until she could get her keys. She was suffering badly from limbo anxiety: you break with the old place, but you're not settled in the new place and there's nothing familiar to diffuse the shock. Then she dropped a box filled with china and busted an heirloom serving tray into shards. The tears rolled.

"What are your most favorite things?" I asked her.

She thought about this, then between sobs, "My grandma's candlesticks."

I cleared everything off the counter that divided the kitchen and living room, located the box they were in, unwrapped them and set them up. Three big silver gothic candleholders. I stuck a yellow candle into each one.

"Better?"

She nodded and I gave her a hug.

When we got everything inside her place she offered to buy me dinner. We went to a seafood place and chatted amicably. Afterward I said, "Hey why don't you come over tomorrow night. I'll make dinner and we'll listen to records."

She hesitated, but accepted.

The following night her eyes kept flitting around my apartment at my belongings: a canvas butterfly chair, a Love and Rockets concert poster, a boxy beige Mac Plus incapable of reaching the dialup internet, a photo of Salvador Dali. I played vintage bossa nova records and prepared fettucine alfredo with chicken. She seemed amused by my primitive second-hand cookware. The great Toulouse-Lautrec spent his time among the prostitutes and alcoholic johns of Parisian beer halls, so there's no shame in weathered Teflon pans.

"They get the job done," I said, "Cooked food is cooked food, right?"

"Absolutely."

Linda studied my drawings for a long time and took a sketch of Garry Shandling (art fair sketches get cash, forgive me) she liked and that I offered to her. Though I hadn't intended to show her my oil series, she wandered into them and ticked through the big dusty canvases.

"Wow," she said, studying them up and down.

"Just wow?"

"Wow is pretty good."

I smiled. "I'll take it from a fellow artist."

She sighed. "Not really. My birdhouses are crap. I should just stop with those things. I carry them around."

"They make you happy."

"Buying a house and living like a proper human being would make me happy."

She gave me a peck as a good night kiss, and from that point I saw her less and less. She travelled incessantly as a public relations person for a corporation, of all things. Pizza delivery flyers and UPS notices collected on her door. Even when she was in town, her hours were erratic and it was hard to catch her. I drew a cartoon of her, surrounded by bird-houses and slid it under her door one night with the inscription: *Just Thinking of You.* The next time I saw her, she was moving out, transferring to Dallas. Two sweaty guys were helping her.

I came to refer to Tarry Hall as Eviction Hall. At least once or twice a month the contents of someone's place ended up on the curb. It amazed me that the owners of the stuff were never around when this happened. No sobbing evicted person ever was there. Others would pick over the books, dressers, clothes, and bric-a-brac. If a couch or bookshelf looked presentable a truck would appear to cart it off. Where were these lost souls? In jail? Deported? Too depressed to care about their stuff? Sometimes mounds of belongings sat for days through rain before garbage men picked up the sogging wet shirts, greeting cards, pillowcases and stuffed animals.

I consider rooting through someone else's stuff bad luck. I never did it.

I once lived in a basement apartment of an older woman's huge house. I had window views of a garden and a parking space in the garage. It was a steal. As quiet as the surface of the moon. At the time, I was doing cartoons for greeting cards. I even brainstormed up an entire set of my own that were bought by a major greeting card company, featuring a nameless character that looked like a giant wart with legs and said things like, "Being with you is like enjoying fresh coffee every morning........and never having to switch to decaf!"

I walked in the garden for inspiration and often came across the old woman sitting at a bench beside her cane. She always pursed her lips, opened her eyes wide and said,

"Hello, hello! Here's the artist!" like Modigliani had just strolled up or I was royalty or something. She was both a patron and a muse. She had a stroke and was put in a nursing home. Relatives wheeled her out to a van telling her platitudes: "You're going to love your new place." She said nothing; the left side of her face drooped. She never looked back at her house of forty years.

The house was sold. The new owners were a middle-aged high-flying executive and his heavy makeup wife. "I really want to stay here," I explained to them, "I illustrate. I create. You should see the work I've done since I've lived here." The vibrations were terrific—unmatched, to this day.

I offered to pay more, but they gave me the boot. They wanted to live in the house alone, no sketchy artists moping around.

Linda's favorite Van Gogh was *Still Life: Sunflowers*, which is one you see a lot in art books. Van Gogh painted it in anticipation of the French painter Gauguin coming to Arles to paint with him in the Yellow House. Van Gogh wanted Gauguin to be part of a community that he envisioned of French painters—part of his attempt to prove himself as a Dutchman among the French. He had high hopes for the place, but the locals turned on him and ran him out of town. After Van Gogh left Arles, he was never quite the same.

It always takes a week or so before you are caught up with where you are living and forget life in the former place. I lived in eight places over my first eighteen years—so I have known about this from an early age. Father flew in the Air Force, which flies planes all over the world and houses families of the fliers in lowly yet passable housing. Even when I left Tarry Hall—after emptying the apartment out completely except for a shoe box and some wire hangers—I had to pause and look around before closing the door the last time. The walls seemed to deserve this. It was not the walls' fault or the closet's fault. They did their best to house me and my things; they stood by, shabby and scarred, passively watching my life without comment. I was sad to leave them at the mercy of others who would come after me.

I check my box at the mail kiosk and the check was not in the mail, as they told me over the phone. I will have to call Chicago about this, and Diana will not be happy. There is a letter that I sent a month ago to Linda, crumpled and stamped Return to Sender. Apparently, she moved from Dallas to parts unknown.

I'm doodling at my drafting table, receiver perched on my shoulder, listening to long distance Muzak. I make loops with my No. 2 pencil, shade the edges—they look like black clouds. I finally get through to my editor in Chicago and ask what is going on. Where is my check?

"We love Arthur," the editor explains. "He's cuddly, like a teddy bear. The kids will love him. It's Arthur's parents. They look scary, like grizzly bears."

"Parents can be scary to kids," I say.

"They're too scary. We need you to make them look like regular bears. Friendlier."

"I need to be paid now. I've got rent to pay."

"We can't pay you until completion. It's in the contract."

I call Diana to tell her of this development, but I'm told she's not at her desk. I stay up all night sketching momma and poppa bears—happy, pudgy angelic bears that even the most skittish child would adore, then overnight mail them to Chicago.

In the morning an envelope is wedged in my front door—a letter from the Windham Gate attorney that formal eviction proceedings start the next day. Letter in one hand, phone in the other, my editor tells me they will send a check via Federal Express and sure enough they do, but they didn't get my address correct on the label so the next day the package sits in the regional office instead of being delivered. I race there and pick up the package, rip it open, deposit the check at the bank, write out a check for rent then drive home.

But when I turn into Windham Gate I'm distracted. Sitting next to the road at the entrance are a couch that looks like my couch, a drafting table that looks like my table and a set of four Van Gogh prints, glass frames gleaming in the sun. *The Cafe Terrace at Arles* propped up next to a coat rack.

Heavens, I think, I've got to get my stuff back inside my apartment before it rains or people in trucks start carting it away. At my door the key doesn't fit into the lock: a shiny new gold deadbolt. I twist the door handle and it refuses to yield. Out by the road, I realize that I have nowhere to put my stuff besides the back seat of my Corolla and there's little room there. I feel panicked that all my stuff is sitting in bags and in stacks around me. My failure at being a responsible member of society makes my face flush. A rumpled armful of clothes slumps over the back of a chair. Packages of charcoal pencils and pastel chalks are scattered on the grass among a toaster and pieces of china. Black plastic bags bulge with untold things.

The canvases of my oil series are scattered atop each other, one propped against a chair: a thickly-stroked cubist explosion of orange paint that absolutely pops in the sunlight. My God, I think, is this a message? Is it time to move into that SoHo loft in Manhattan and get serious about oil painting and getting into galleries? The reality of having gray, underscored clouds over my head instead of a roof is the more pressing matter, and this fevered dream passes.

I sit on one end of the couch, hand on my forehead, weeds poking up between my feet. Cars glide through the entrance and on past, the drivers not looking at me. I sort through a miasma of thoughts: it would be nice to go back to my place to relax for a bit to better deal with this. If it rains, everything I own will be soaked—a lifetime chain of orderly moves from one place to the next has been broken.

I'm outside the system now, I keep thinking. Outside the system. In a life imitates art twist, I'm now Arthur lost in the woods.

But I can't stomach the thought of looking for another place and beginning the process over again. It's a sunny day and my stuff is partially in the shade of a tree. There is a soft breeze. My head sinks back into a cushion. It is actually quite a beautiful day. I look at the shrubs and flowers around me. In the stillness I feel like one of them. In nature the flowers are in one spot and a hydrangea plant sits in another, an oak seedling grows in another and they never worry about where they are, or someone ripping them up at the roots, taking them away. Why shouldn't they be happy? They have everything they need. But we will never be planted.

We are born with two legs.

A man wearing a gas company shirt wanders over and picks up *Still Life: Sunflowers*, studies it and puts it under his arm. Am I invisible? I start to say something, but then I realize that it will be one less thing to worry about, one less thing to house. With his free hand he opens a folder of my drawings and flips through them. "That's enough," I tell him. He closes the folder and walks away.

I get the urge to march over to the leasing office and tell Diana just what she can do with her phony community when a potential storyline for my book hits me and stops me cold: the llama, the python and the space alien all get stabbed in the back by other creatures, kicked in the butt, banished from paradise, but they put their heads together and make a valiant comeback. They buy an old Ford van—the kind electric utility companies use, plenty of room in the back for their stuff—and tear off across the country for the adventure of their lives. They drive wherever they want, park wherever they damn well please, and nobody can touch them because they own the van. They drive it till the wheels fall off and buy more wheels. They cross desert and prairie, sticking their heads out the window while driving, yelling at the top of their lungs, their voices echoing across the landscape.

Sounds great, doesn't it?

The breeze picks up. The branches above me shift and filter the sunlight. Natural light really is the best for drawing. America is a very big place. Lots of wide open spaces. Of course, nothing is that simple, unless you're a kid.

SPACE FOOD

I t's weird to think back about all of it. I spent much of my youth sweating in the backseat of a Chevrolet Grand Safari station wagon, staring out the window at the generic pine tree line of an interstate highway and wondering when we would arrive at the house of a distant relative. Summer was the visiting season. Every weekend we drove somewhere. My father ran the air conditioning, but my mother would turn it to the lowest setting to get better gas mileage. After an hour of the sun beating down on the car, the meager wisps of cool air were overwhelmed by hot air from the cargo area. When we visited my cousin Ray Ray in 1976, that year of Bicentennial celebration, I was ten years old, full of questions and hotter than usual.

I was ready to go that morning at the appointed hour, in sneakers and shorts. My mother walked into my room in a tasteful dress and broach. I was adding my latest scale model to the collection of meticulously painted and decaled dive bombers and helicopters that hung from my ceiling in a perpetual dogfight. Stooping slightly, wary of a jet fighter lodging in her hair, she told me to put on my Sunday clothes. My face drooped. We were driving to another state in early August and it would be hot enough without the monkey suit.

"We're going to have a sit-down dinner there," she said, in explanation of the clothing.

"Why?"

"Ray Ray's been having a hard time. He needs our support."

The correlation between one's earnestness and the precision of one's dress had reared its gilded head. It was the right thing, like sending a personalized thank you note for every gift received and the necessity of young people learning dances such as the foxtrot and waltz. According to my mother, a prolific organizer of dinner parties and a longtime Library Authority board member, the decent people of the world identified each other by these graces. I believed her.

With dull submission, I opened my closet. There hung the blue polyester blend slacks, the gray J.C. Penney jacket and the stain proof Junior collection tie. Below them, in a protective cardboard box, sat polished black leather shoes with silver buckles, the most expensive items entrusted to my care. I wore them infrequently, and they were stiff and unforgiving when I did. It was necessary to have pristine and shiny footwear in God's House. The Lord frowned upon ratty Chuck Taylor All Stars.

I pulled on the black socks that matched the shoes

and took the trousers off the hanger. My Father peered into my room to ensure I was getting with the program. In his ubiquitous gray suit, he was always ready to go either to church or his optometry office. Even on Saturdays he read the newspaper wearing a tie and an ultra-starched shirt which rustled as he spread open the paper. He flashed a thumbs up and clicked his tongue. Looking at my mirrored self wearing the scratchy jacket and pants I felt a small bump of pride and made a wish I could one day match my father's suited swagger.

I tried to jump in the car tie in hand. Not a clip-on, the real thing. My plan was to fashion a perfect Windsor knot when we arrived, but Mother made me do it in the house. The car was for traveling, not dressing—something only low class people did, like eating dinner barefoot. The world is so clear cut when you're a kid and, for a while, it's wonderful.

I didn't mind the trips. It seemed an important thing to do, like we were diplomats.

It took three hours to drive to Ray Ray's house. It wasn't his real name. He was related to my mother somehow and when he was a child some other child in the family called him Ray Ray. It stuck.

The sun shone through the window on my side of the car, my legs broiling within the synthetic slacks. I loosened my tie and ran my hand over spots that my mother, even after tenacious scrubbing, could not make disappear. I stared out the window and read signs. Why did they always advertise peaches and boiled peanuts?

Who cared about these things? I asked Father.

Pausing from whistling and steering wheel tapping, he looked in the rearview mirror and said with his usual calm assuredness. "It's a way of getting people to stop and buy things. If they stop to look at peaches, they might buy gas or something else."

To my amazement, he had an answer for everything. His shirt collar lay snug against his shaved neck. Mother had on a round, velvety hat with netting over it. Jewels were stuck in the netting, caught like flies.

To pass the time, I brought the W volume of the World Book Encyclopedia with me because I was into warfare—specifically, WWII. I memorized tiny maps covered with black arrows and felt enthralled that during this period the world was engulfed in a match between good and evil. Entire economies were converted to churn out B-17 bombers, Sherman tanks and the dreaded Messerschmitt ME 109 fighter plane. Men wrote in diaries in the mud of Guadalcanal and jumped out of airplanes over other countries. All activity in my house paled in comparison.

My parents purchased the encyclopedia set for me from a door-to-door salesman because they figured it would encourage reading and the accumulation of knowledge—attributes of responsible people. It worked. The books fascinated me and tore me away from reruns of *The Munsters* and *The Partridge Family*. They had something to say about everything, but my favorite topics were things like Voodoo, the Loch Ness Monster and

WWII, choices which concerned my parents. They had expected me to bone up on Benjamin Franklin and Thomas Jefferson. An encyclopedia can be a dangerous thing. It gives a version of events, a set of explanations that beg more questions. If the Bible is the most widely read book, who wrote it? If Hindus believe in reincarnation, then why don't Presbyterians? Why did Lee Harvey Oswald shoot Kennedy?

I studied a picture of the battleship Bismarck in the *World Book*, then slapped the book shut. "Why does Ray Ray need our support?" I pictured us lifting him over our heads.

"Some of us need more support than others because some of us are less fortunate in the world," Mother said. Family was like that. Things were squishy. Whatever Ray Ray's problems, I understood it was a delicate matter that could easily dissolve into hard feelings. Years before, Father had gotten a series of phone calls involving Ray Ray and money—either him trying to round up money from family or family rounding up money for him. I wasn't sure which. Father talked in the library with the doors closed and emerged with a pained expression. Mother would often say, "Sometimes it's a treat and sometimes it's a chore, but it's the only family you'll ever have."

"What does Ray Ray do?" I put my feet up on the seat and laid my head on the vibrating door armrest, careful to avoid the ash tray jammed with old gum.

Mother looked to Father for this one. "Ray Ray is

something of a journeyman," he said. "I think now he has a lawn mower repair business."

"What's wrong with lawn mower repair?"

"There's nothing wrong with it. There are many ways to make an honest living. Every man has to be respected for his way." He started to say something, then stopped. "Some of us are more diligent at applying ourselves than others, however," he added.

Here's what I didn't know back then: This would be the only time we visited Ray Ray. Afterward, we reported to other family members about how he was doing, definitive experts on the subject for a long while. Years later when we got a call that he had died, Mother would say with a degree of satisfaction, "You remember visiting Ray Ray, don't you?"

We turned off the highway and drove down back roads with farmland and scattered homes. It wasn't a subdivision, like where we lived, but just randomly placed older, crumbling houses with neglected Big Wheels and tricycles nesting in weedy yards. My mother turned around and looked at me. She pitched her forehead forward and frowned slightly. "Ray Ray will be glad to see us," she said, "and we'll certainly be pleased to see him. He's had an interesting life."

"Ray Ray served in the military and was in Korea during the war," Father said, looking in the mirror again.

Mother shook her head, "That isn't a good subject to bring up. Some things are best unmentioned." She looked at her watch.

I had never seen his house before and couldn't guess which would be his. We stopped in front of a single level cinder-block house with no trees or shrubs around it. It was off-white with a hint of gray and the windows had no shutters—a tropical looking house. The yard had patches of brown, vine-like grass interspersed among stretches of sand.

We stepped out of the car into the oven-like midday sun. Father buttoned his jacket and Mother straightened her dress. Ray Ray appeared at the side of the house holding a sprinkler, pulling a hose behind him. "How was that ride?" he yelled, jerking and wrestling with the hose.

"Just fine," Father said.

Ray Ray trudged across the yard in a blue jump suit—thick wrinkled neck, barrel chest, short legs. He reminded me of a bulldog. He put one knee on the ground, screwed the hose onto the end of the sprinkler and set it down. He wiped the sweat off his brow with a handkerchief and pushed his steamed horn-rimmed glasses up his nose.

We stood on the cement path that led to the front door, squinting in bright light.

"Did you take highway 52?" he asked, looking up suddenly.

"We took I-25 to 71," Father said.

Ray Ray nodded. "Six of one, half dozen of another." He walked to the side of the house and a tall ray of water sprung into the air from the sprinkler. Droplets hit the dirt around the hose, then moved toward us as the sprinkler pivoted. We shuffled toward the house to avoid the water that threatened overhead.

Ray Ray shook hands with my Father and kissed my Mother. "Helen, you look beautiful and lovely, as always."

"Hello, sir," I said, offering a firm handshake—the mark of a gentleman.

"Young Ted," he clamped my fingers with an impossibly large hand. "You're growing like a weed. You playing football?" He had short bristly hair on the top of his head.

"Right now I'm taking tennis lessons."

Ray Ray stared at me as though he had never heard the word 'tennis' before.

Ray Ray opened the screen door and ushered us into the house. Dark, it smelled like the inside of a seashell. Faint music crackled somewhere inside the house.

"Who wants a sip of water? Some good ole H2O?" he asked, leading us into the kitchen. He tossed ice cubes into a cloudy glass, handed it to Mother and nodded toward the faucet. Faded drapes hung over every window, leaving the interior in twilight.

"I'm so very glad you came to see me. Edward," he motioned to my Father, "Let me show you something I'm working on. Then I'll get that dinner going."

When they left, Mother turned on an overhead light in the kitchen. "Oh, dear," she whispered, lifting a pan from a fetid stack in the sink. She opened the refrigerator. No light came on inside. She peered within.

Ray Ray chattered in another room, clearing his throat occasionally. I left the kitchen and walked down a hall, wary that some large dog might jump out of the shadows and bite me. A lamp shaped like an eagle illuminated a small room with a television set and some bookcases with thick, well-thumbed paperbacks. A plaque on the wall read:

> *Recognition of Meritorious and Distinguished Service*
> United States Army
> Korean Conflict
> Presented to: Rafford Jacob Smalls

Two bayonets, crossed over each other, were mounted on the same wall. The steel blades had a dull bluish finish, the serrated handles cold to the touch. Had Ray Ray jabbed an enemy soldier in the stomach with them? Did they once drip with blood? I knew nothing of what happened in Korea or why the plaque referred to it as a conflict. I pictured Ray Ray charging up a beach on Sicily, dodging Nazi gunfire—an image that I knew was probably flawed, but I couldn't picture Korea. I hadn't read that far in the encyclopedia. I had the most enormous desire to take one of the bayonets and spirit it away in my jacket.

Back in the kitchen, my parents watched Ray Ray open cabinets which contained dusty jars and boxes. Mother said, "Ray Ray, we would hate to put you to a lot of trouble to make dinner." She touched him on the forearm. "Why don't we go to a nice restaurant?"

He looked at us and thought deeply about this proposition. A strip of paper now peeked out of Ray Ray's back pocket, light green, the color of my parent's checks. His eyes lit up. "We could eat some barbecue over at the Cedar Wagon."

"Wonderful," Mother said.

"That sounds like a winner," Father said.

"What do you say, Ted?" Ray Ray placed his heavy hand on my shoulder.

"Sounds good to me."

"Then it's agreed," he said. He slapped his hands together and laughed, his voice echoing and booming throughout the kitchen. I felt fearful of him. Another cousin of mine had told me that Ray Ray had gone to prison for selling stolen goods. He was caught by the Sheriff in an undercover operation and sent to the big house where he learned to pick locks. I asked my Father about this. He raised his eyebrows and said, "Don't believe everything you hear," which was confusing enough that I knew it was probably true.

Something clanged hard against the floor in another room—a dagger? Everyone looked alarmed. I braced for an investigation and questioning. Ray Ray shrugged and laughed, as though metal objects crashing to the floor were commonplace in his house.

Ray Ray changed into slacks and a knit shirt with a breast pocket for his glasses case. We walked with him behind the house where he shut the door of an aluminum garage which reeked of oil stains and cut grass. Lawn mowers, bicycles, weed trimmers, post hole diggers and assorted mechanical parts were crowded in there. "This here's my inner sanctum. Where I keep my secrets," he said with a grin. He secured the door with a combination lock.

We drove in our wagon. No cars were parked around his house. He sat in the back seat and told us how lawn mower repair wasn't a business of the future but a business of the past, since lawn mowers were going electric. The business world was always changing and he was going to change with it.

"Titanium is the strongest metal there is," he said.

"Doesn't NASA use that in spacecraft?" Father said.

"They do. That's why it's being used for television antennas. Install a titanium antenna on your roof and it won't blow down even in a hurricane. Also, the reception is superior." He looked at me, his eyes huge behind his glasses. "That's why I'm going full speed ahead with my installation business."

"Sounds terrific Ray," Father said, "you've got a jump on it."

"We could use one. Maybe you could give us a deal," Mother said.

"Consider it done." Ray Ray kept shifting back and forth in his seat, leaning over the front seat to tell my father where to turn, pointing out the window at landmarks, humming when he wasn't talking, tapping on his knees. His fidgeting made me nervous.

"You must be hot in that monkey suit," he said to me.

"I sure am." My back was on fire.

"Then shed that sport coat."

I took off my jacket and disentangled the tie. Dressing up for Ray Ray and his smelly cement block house now seemed absurd. Mother glanced at me briefly, but said nothing. I placed the jacket in the cargo area.

Ray Ray eagerly told us about another one of his ventures. He was currently seeking investors. Buoyed by interest in the space program and the success of Tang, he envisioned an entire line of "Space Food." Ray Ray was purchasing large quantities of vegetables, pulverizing them in a contraption he had invented himself called The Pulverizer—he was considering patenting it—and pouring the resulting vege-mush into plastic pouches that were hermetically sealed. There were spoilage problems. Grocery stores were hesitant. The project was before its time, he claimed. "Presentation considerations are still very important to people when they eat. In the future this will change."

I had read about The Manhattan Project and I knew some innovations took time. Even the most brilliant scientists in the world: Oppenheimer, Bohr, Fermi, and Teller needed three solid years working in the desert at Los Alamos before they perfected the atomic bomb. The Space Food sounded convenient; it had that going for it.

At the Cedar Wagon we all ate pork ribs, as Ray Ray strongly insisted. "It is the only way to experience the *true essence* of this place." Ray Ray raised his arms and proudly pointed at farm memorabilia that dotted the wall and provided an ambiance.

Holding an upside-down bottle of sauce, he positioned it over Mother's plate. "Helen, you absolutely must try their sauce!"

"Oh no. I can't." She was allergic to ketchup.

"Just a little itty bit."

"No thank you, Ray."

He spurted out a healthy crimson button next to her mashed potatoes then retreated. He talked about his Uncle Dennis, a daredevil aviator who went broke and became permanently grounded when he married the wrong woman. "When I was a boy, Dennis used to take me out to the airport. He taught me a lot about planes."

When the check came Ray Ray grabbed it from the waitress then pulled out his alligator hide wallet. "Edward, I insist."

"Ray, that's not necessary to do," Father said.

"No, siree Bob." He sprung from the booth, colliding with a waitress.

At his request we stopped by the airport. We parked at the end of a fenced runway.

Single and double prop planes buzzed towards us and lifted over our heads. Ray Ray, Father and I cheered when the big double props lifted off after coming farthest down the runway towards us, their engines roaring and deafening overhead. Mother put her fingers in her ears and crouched.

Ray Ray spread his arms out to the side, like wings,

and explained to me how planes fly. "The propeller pulls the plane forward through the air. The air rushing over the top of the wing moves faster than the air underneath the wing, giving it lift." He craned his neck forward and shuffled his feet like he was about to take off. My parents glanced at each other, trying to stifle laughter.

"I thought the propeller gave the plane lift," I said.

"Common misconception. It's the shape of the wings. It takes a leap of faith before you get it."

We stood looking through the fence, our fingers locked into the chain link, waiting for the next plane. We were out of ear shot of my parents. I asked him, "Did you fly when you were in Korea?"

He scrunched up one of his eyes, looked down at me then ahead at the parked planes. "No, sir. I was a grunt, a foot soldier. I would have had an easier time of it if I had been a flyboy, I'll tell you that." He shook his head sadly. He thought about it longer then said quietly, "Would have stayed warmer. Might have saved some toes."

Frostbite? Had the enemy shot off his toes?

I got up some courage. All my reading seemed to require me to ask: "Over in Korea, did you kill anyone?"

Ray Ray tilted his head back slightly. A dazed look passed over his face and his shoulders dropped. He said in a slow, distant way: "That's the real question, isn't it?" He took out his handkerchief and wiped his neck. "When you're in a war," he said, "you have to do some things." He looked at me to gauge my reaction and if I had a recognition of what his answer meant.

I thought a moment, then nodded once.

A plane sputtered into position well down the runway. It pointed toward us, the engine whine building until it skimmed over our heads. It seemed to revive Ray Ray.

"Looky here at this." He pulled the end of one of his fingers, a ring finger I think, separating it at the joint, leaving a scarred, waving nub half the size of the others. With his good hand, he held the fake finger like a match, turned it slowly before my eyes, then popped it back on the nub. I couldn't breathe. I studied his hands the rest of the day, trying to figure out which one was fake. I couldn't find a seam or one that looked disfigured, though one appeared straighter than the others.

The next day, I told Father about this. He laughed, insisting it was a skillful trick. No other relatives from that generation I've asked have confirmed that he had a fake digit or remembered anything about it. But I know what I saw.

Though I was still bursting with curiosity, I refrained from asking Ray Ray if he had machine gunned or bayoneted any of the enemy. I let it go. I suspected that war wasn't the grand chess match that the encyclopedia dryly recounted: this Armored Division prevailed here; this side won that battle. With every explosion fingers were being minced off by the shrapnel, and worse.

Father discreetly looked at his watch and glanced at Mother with a look that said: *It's getting late Helen. Time to pack up the wagon.* Eyebrows raised, she nodded, signaling agreement.

"Say, they're building a new mall!" Ray Ray said to all of us, shouting above the din of a plane landing on an opposite runway. "It's going to be an indoor shopping mall with over thirty different stores—a big department store, and this area with little restaurants where you can get food." Hands on his hips, certain he had our full attention. "They're putting it up right now over in Tolarville and it's really going to be *something*. Let's go take a look."

"That sounds great," I said with sincerity.

Father gave in. "We'll go."

In the car I realized Korea wasn't that sore a subject with Ray Ray. In all, he was doing pretty good. Between the titanium antennas and the Space Food, he had ideas galore. He was on the verge of something. He didn't seem to need lifting. Not that I thought my parents had lied. I just knew what I knew. Knowledge is the jet fuel of the universe. It can cause a person to do lots of things, like drink an entire fifth of bourbon at the prom and chip your front tooth on a toilet, or quit college after two semesters, or spend a year taking photographs of Buddhists, beggars and sunsets in Katmandu, or play poker professionally for the last seven years, winning and losing outrageous sums of money (Mother refuses to acknowledge that last one).

We turned off the highway and onto a dirt road and drove toward the construction site, tires crunching over rocks and pebbles. No trees, just stumps and roots sticking up from churned earth. Like the place had been bombed. The dirt path became pavement and we glided across a new black tar parking lot. Light poles flitted past. The mall came into view, a skeletal ghost town. As I climbed out of the Grand Safari, a thick layer of white clouds blocked out the afternoon sun. The place smelled of lumber, which sat around in stacks, covered by plastic wrapping that crinkled in the breeze. We walked across the newly poured tar—hard but sticky on the soles of our shoes—to a cement curb that formed a boundary between us and the metal girders and two by fours that Ray Ray pointed to as the mall in creation.

"There she is," he said, waving his fists in front of him.

What I noticed was mud everywhere, like the mall had been dropped from the sky after a flood. But there was something majestic, expectant about the place.

"Around the corner over there," he pointed and made a pecking motion with his finger, "they are putting in a fountain that will be at the entrance to one of the department stores." He stepped over the curb and started down a lumber strip walkway laid over the muddy red clay, the boards caked with dry bits. He looked back at us.

"Ray, I'm not sure I want to get any closer than this," Mother said, her arms crossed, standing in her pumps. Father put his hands around her and rubbed her shoulders.

"What do you say, young Ted?" Ray Ray asked.

"Let's go," I said. Expressions on my parents' faces that they wanted to say something, but wouldn't.

I liked the idea of surveying this work in progress, spying on what the construction workers were doing. I walked behind Ray Ray on a double set of boards that went over a small hill and hugged close to the building. I unbuttoned my cuffs and rolled up my sleeves to feel more rugged. Cement flooring had been poured inside around steel girders. Plastic rustled inside the structure. The smell of fiberglass and lumber wafted from the darkness as we tromped down the path.

Around a corner, out of sight of my parents, we crossed an open lot where earth had turned to mud, the mud drying with imprints of giant knobby tires and footprints. The walkway stopped at the edge of this lot.

"That's the fountain there." He pointed to what looked like a cement pond, a low wall circling the edges. He stepped off the edge of the last plank into the mire and made his way over to the fountain, each step making a sucking noise as he pulled his feet out of the mud. I stood at the end of the boards and looked at the mud, which had a thin dry upper layer and a wet mushy under layer.

The fountain was still yards away! I stretched my neck to see, painfully conscious of my footwear. Every fiber of my being tensed. A dizzy sensation swept over me. Ray Ray gestured that I should come over, but I cannot blame him for what I did. Even without the motion, I would have stepped off anyway. But who can know these things for sure? Mud pushed around the soles and over the tops of my black leather Sunday school shoes, like a thick reddish-brown frosting. I took several shifting, precarious steps toward Ray Ray and stood beside him as he crouched and ran his hand along the low wall of the fountain. It had a smooth white finish and open-ended pipes. The size of a small swimming pool, no debris or dirt marred its expanse.

He stood, put his hands on his hips and looked toward the facade of an entrance. "This place is going to be so new, so beautiful, that people are going to come just to see the inside of it. People will come by the truckload and walk around inside all day. This is *the* future. And that's God's own truth."

Looking inside the dim mall past hanging wires and stacks of drywall, I imagined people coming there, walking across pavement and brick, admiring the fountain, then on through gleaming doors to spend money in the shops. It was hard to picture at first. It took a leap of faith—and then I saw that it all would happen.

"That's the way I see it," he said, "despite what the opinions of other people will be. Because if you can't believe in something, then you're nothing."

HANK'S PLACE

Tina, my wife's perennially troubled friend, invited us over for dinner. She's one of those women who drag around a cosmic disfavor which has doomed her to a series of dreadful sagas with a collection of marginal, sadistic guys. After divorcing her last husband she ended up with the house. It's in a subdivision where Jessica and I once lived when we got married seven years ago: identical 1960's ranch houses with carports. Starter homes, if you don't mind the lived-in odor. Jessica tells me about Tina's latest man as we drive, a guy with a paying job who's never been in jail, so expectations are sky high. Jessica is like Tina in that respect. Hope dwells in every crack and crevice.

We don't park in the driveway because a fat tire, cobalt blue Dodge Charger with a rusted, piecemeal tailpipe is parked there.

"Is that Mr. Wonderful's hot rod?" I say, eyeing the vintage muscle car.

"His name is Chuck," Jessica says in a cautionary way.

"As in, chuck wagon?"

Poised for social discourse, she ignores the comment. We disagreed about coming over. I've been in a funk lately, in no mood to put on the happy face. Plus, Tina's impositions on Jessica are shocking. This is a stubborn high school friendship strained to absurdist limits. Phone sessions at one AM? Are you kidding me?

Tina works at a car dealership and Jessica and I are now doing stuff like flying to Thailand on behalf of my employer, a software company. I'm part of a management culture getting free lattes and ping pong to unleash problem solving skills. We live in a recently built stucco fortress in a desirable exurb. What man can walk away from such a house, sunlight flashing off brass fixtures, his wife biting her bottom lip, eyes moist, the place beaming with infinite promise, as though it existed just for us? There wasn't anything wrong with our old house. My parents have lived in the same house most of their lives. Roof. Plumbing. Good enough. But the stucco called, for a price, and it takes most of my take home pay. Its actual price is a tension, an ever-present knowing that my financial solvency is bound up staying employed at the software company.

I get out of the car and realize I'm overdressed: loafers, pressed slacks and a black silk jacket that Jessica bought for me cheap in Thailand. An outfit more suited to sipping single malt scotch or being onstage in Las Vegas than attending a ranch house get together.

Tina opens the door with puffy, bloodshot eyes and

greets us with a voice strained from trauma, a bashful smile. She puts her hands together at her heart—our presence a blessing—and gives us both hugs.

"There's a delay making dinner," she says softly, "because of a problem running water in the sink." She brushes back her dark curly bangs and puts a hand on her forehead.

A booming male voice contorted by echo comes from the kitchen. "Can't believe you don't have a proper wrench but that's typical." The *tink tink* of metal against pipe. Sounds like he's under the sink. "This fucker couldn't open a jelly jar."

"Chuck, they just walked in the door," she yells over her shoulder. "Come out here."

Jessica whispers to Tina, *Are you all right?* Tina shakes her head and describes how water leaked all over the kitchen floor. They walk together over to the couch and sit. We did things with Tina and her former husband. He sold cars and seemed like a decent guy, then he got another woman pregnant.

In the kitchen, Chuck is bent over looking into the refrigerator. Wearing jeans, no shirt. Thick, tanned neck and back. "Never a goddamn thing in here," he says in a low voice. He reaches toward the back then snaps his head around quickly at me. "Want one?"

"One what?"

He pulls out a beer can and holds it toward me, still half-inside the refrigerator.

"Sure."

He tosses one to me, pops the top on his can and

closes the door. He points to the open area under the sink. "Leaky u-pipe. Took out the old one. Can't put another one in with this shit for tools."

"I'm Bill." I offer a handshake.

"Oh, hey sorry." He wipes his hand on the thigh of his jeans and shakes my hand. "Nice to meet you." Twangy, monotone voice, like he's never pleased to meet anyone. He smells of pit odor and cigarettes. Dark hair slicked back behind his ears and remote, determined eyes.

"Could I help somehow?" I ask. An insincere offer given my outfit. I feel like a preppie homeowner supervising a plumber.

"Not unless you got a wrench in your pocket." He reaches for a denim shirt hung over a chair and starts buttoning it from the bottom up. Chuck reminds me of the guys I worked with the summer during college, when I poured tar with a road crew—tough, but with a kind of brooding boredom that makes them hard to read.

Tina appears in the doorway with her hands on her hips. "Can I finally use the sink now?" Implying it's all Chuck's fault.

He glares at her, arms crossed and doesn't move a muscle. "I keep telling you. I need the right tool," he says through his teeth.

"Well, could you do that?"

"I could call my brother."

"Please do that." Tina turns and walks away.

Chuck looks at me for a reaction. I take a long sip on the beer, the aluminum aftertaste smarting in the back of my throat, then grin at Chuck. He shakes his head. "That woman's on my very last nerve." He puts down his beer, picks up the receiver to the wall-mounted phone and dials. "Hank, it's me. Gotta borrow a wrench. I'm coming over."

Chuck and I walk into the living room. Jessica is patting Tina on the knee in a consoling way—their collective dream dashed once again. Chuck says he's going to pick up a wrench. He tucks in his shirt, fishing his hand around the front of his jeans.

"That's fine. We do have plenty of time," Jessica says with excessive cheer. She looks at me. "Maybe you could go with Chuck."

Our taxi driver, a man who may or may not have known English, dropped off Jessica and me on the wrong side of Bangkok. It took us hours to realize this. In a three-piece wool suit, ready to press the flesh at our hotel with chain-smoking dignitaries from multinational conglomerates, I stood next to our luggage in a swath of sunlight that seemed focused through a giant magnifying glass. Motor scooters buzzed around me, one knocking over a garment bag. I waved my arms to attract another taxi. Sandal wearing people smiled shyly at me as I chanted our hotel name. Royal Phuket? Royal Phuket! Jessica, in a sundress, ran back and forth across the street, touching wares, haggling with vendors, children running around her.

She returned with a strange purplish fruit. This should be delicious! A wiry fellow with an eye patch looked over our luggage. An old woman dumped a plate of entrails onto the street. I was late to meet the chain-smoking dignitaries. Would they stick around?

In frustration, I swung my jacket at a passing scooter. Relax, Jessica said. Look around. It's beautiful here.

The sun is going down. We take Chuck's vintage Charger. I settle into the passenger seat.

"I didn't have to offer to fix her sink," Chuck says, fuming.

"Now you're in it."

He turns over the engine and backs down the drive. The big lumbering V-8 chugs steadily with a round, even sound. It's in good shape. He pulls down the gear shift into Drive. "I don't even know why I'm with her. She acts like I'm her husband. If I was smart I'd be dating her sister. Have you met Christie?"

"I have." She came to our old house once with Tina. Long red hair and long tan legs. The car salesman got drunk once and made a pass at Christie, who reported the infraction to Tina.

Chuck whistles. "She could be a damn swimsuit model. She'd be awfully hard to turn away, know what I mean?" I'm not going to say anything that could be taken as agreeing that I have the hots for Christie or would under the right circumstances.

Chuck says: "She could eat Ritz with runny peanut butter, and I wouldn't kick her off my Serta."

It takes me a second to realize it's a variation of not kicking someone out of bed for eating crackers. I laugh, despite myself. He laughs too—deep and rapid, like a buzzer sounding over and over.

He turns onto a four-lane road and guns the engine. It lets out a full growl: a hearty sound of fuel and air combustion that affirms cars are machines. It reminds me of my Dad's guzzler cars. Jessica and I have late model Japanese sedans that only give a faint hum if pushed.

"What do you do for a living Bill?" Chuck glances at me out of the corner of his eye.

"I work for a software company." Junior Vice President for Marketing, but I'm not going to rub it in. "And you?"

"I got a business laying tile."

"Just you?"

"These days I have a new assistant. He takes every dime he makes and mails it back to Costa Rica." Chuck props his left arm on his door and winds ruffles his sleeve. "You don't find many like him anymore."

At a stoplight Chuck reaches under his seat and pulls out a cassette, flicks aside the plastic and pops it in the stereo. From the spaceship cover I can tell it's Boston's first album. My brother Ralph, older by three years but a different generation, had the album in high school. His generation, the tail end boomers, with their love of 70s arena rock, *M.A.S.H.*, *National Lampoon* magazine and brushed neck length hair. I listened to Boston and the rest of Ralph's record collection before gravitating toward new wave bands like Devo and the Cars. The music comes on in the middle of "Peace of Mind" during the soaring guitar solo I've always liked.

Chuck bobs his head.

A scratching noise comes from the back seat, a frantic rustling, and a putrid smell tweaks my nostrils. There's a wooden box on the back seat with a hinged lid, a locked clasp, and thin slits between vertical posts. A dark form moves within.

"What's in the box?" I ask.

"Did you know rats can eat through cardboard, even plywood? That box is pressure treated wood. They *still* gnaw around inside." He smiles and shakes his head. Will rats never cease to amaze?

"Unusual pet."

"No, Albert is my pet. He's a Burmese python. That rat's gonna be dinner."

"How big a snake?"

"Probably near eight feet. The more you feed them the bigger they get. I keep Albert in a phone booth turned sideways." He takes his hands off the wheel to illustrate an object turning sideways. "Can't really take him out anymore. When they get big, they get ornery. He wrapped around my second wife's leg. Took me an hour to get it off."

"No kidding."

"All true."

I get the feeling Chuck is telling the truth. He's the kind of guy who tells a story with a boring end or exciting end because that's what happened, or, if he's mad at you, he looks you in the eye and says you're a son of a bitch. It's refreshing.

My boss at the software company, the CEO,

Jerry—everyone calls him Jere—is from the West Coast. Jerry wears colorful sweaters and says things like, "Tell accounting to cool out." He praises employees as he fires them. Afterward, they're panicked as to whether they've been promoted or terminated. He's big on personal development and demands that everyone around him personally develop, so as to synergize workplace excellence.

The other day he dropped a bamboo sword on my desk, spilling coffee. I covered my phone receiver. "This is the *shinai*," he said carefully. "Kendo is a discipline that dates back to the Samurai warriors. Those guys knew focus." He's wearing an armored skirt and a protective breastplate.

"I see."

"It's super good at character building and learning controlled aggression."

"I'm on the phone to Singapore."

"I've signed up you and Jonathan and Larissa. It's a must for your work section."

What's wrong with softball? Must we beat each other over the head? Some of my cohorts think Jerry is a ditz, but I know it's all ass covering. Screw up and he says you didn't do it his way, cut a big deal and he says his strategy worked beautifully. I've adopted his elliptical language patterns to battle him: I'm positive about the target date, but I have concerns.

At Hank's place, there are a million cars in the front yard. Dusk is settling. It's a neighborhood zoned for light industrial, an auto glass place down the street. Hank's house apparently doubles as his business venue. We drive through a chain link fence topped with razor wire. When I step out of the car, two mixed breed hounds sniff the back of my hand with twitchy circumspection. In twilight I follow Chuck beside the house—voices of a woman and a kid talking inside—to a huge ramshackle steel garage at the back of the lot.

I can't guess the entrance until Chuck pulls a panel, and a door swings open. Spotlights are rigged from the ceiling: it's as bright as the inside of a lamp shade. Hoses, tailpipes and gears hang from the walls. Reminds me of the shed my Dad worked in. He worked for the water authority and over-hauled cars in his spare time. A faint perfume of oil, clutch fluid and old tires usually trailed him. I never liked mechanical stuff, but Ralph was a natural and worked with Dad.

"This is Bill," Chuck says to Hank, a burly guy in a dark, greasy jumpsuit, wiping his hands with a towel. Hank looks at me and nods. A truck without a hood is in the center of the garage. An engine block suspended by chains hangs over the engine bay. My eye picks up a slight swing.

"Since you're here you can help me with something," Hanks says to Chuck, and I guess me too. He points to the engine block. Chuck calls me over to the controls of a hydraulic crane and shows me the appropriate lever.

"Go easy with it," he says.

"Is that block new?" I ask Hank, just to say something.

"It's reconditioned. Don't tell anybody that." He smiles.

I take off my jacket and put it on a dark wooden bench on an uncluttered spot. Chuck and Hank put their hands on either side of the engine. Easy does it, I hear my father say. I work the lever in steady incremental pulls.

We all let out a sigh of relief when it's in snug. I'm thankful the chains didn't snap and no hands were crushed. Chuck and I hover around the bumper while Hank secures the engine with bolts. Hank straightens his back, stuffs his rag into his pocket and pulls out a half-smoked joint, pinching it with his thick fingers. He lights it, sucks and passes it to Chuck who makes the end glow and passes it to me. The smoke is harsh and hot. I pass it back to Hank and wonder about the last time I did this. It was years ago when I visited Ralph.

I pick up my jacket and notice glistening spots on a sleeve and oil drops on the bench. *Dammit.* It's 8:30 and dinner is nowhere in sight. It's pitch black when I step outside. Crickets chirp in a thicket of grasses. Stars are out. I get the odd feeling looking toward the house that I have no idea where I am, or what's lurking and rustling among the weeds.

Somehow, it's a good feeling.

There is no way to get into a car like the Charger without

sensing the car's malice, its sneer. The low-slung bucket seats, indestructible dashboard, the heavy *thunk* of the steel door like a bank vault swinging shut. There's also the aroma of vinyl gone through hard duty, food bits rolled under the seats, air fresheners from years gone by and in this case, one defiant rodent clawing again in protest.

Chuck slams his door and hands me a pipe wrench. He puts the key in the ignition, then reaches behind his seat and pulls out a square-shaped bottle: Jim Beam. He takes a long draw then looks at me. "Yes? Maybe?"

It's rather juvenile to drink in a car, but I figure it's part of the flow. I take a healthy gulp and pass it back. I detect an unusual lemony flavor within the palate hints of toasted almond. "That stuff tastes funky. It's gone bad."

Chuck fills the car with his stutter laugh. "That's cause it's not bourbon. It was when I bought the bottle, but when I finished it, I made my own concoction."

"A concoction?" Warm ripples cross my frontal lobe.

"A little whiskey, little red wine, and some special ingredients." He nestles the bottle behind his seat.

"What's in the secret sauce?"

He shakes his head, a sheepish grin. "It's a secret."

"Tell." My toes are tingly.

"I add a little vinegar. And, it's practically microscopic proportions, but I add some VCR cleaner to add a twist, give it some kick."

"Oh, yeah?"

"Yeah."

Great. I've just self-induced a lobotomy. But whatever was in the juice, he drank it too so it shouldn't be fatal. I'll just end up back at the dinner party with my face contorted like a twisted drop out kid at a Grateful Dead concert. Actually, I'm feeling pretty good. It seems to be working *for* me.

Dinner will come in its own sweet time.

Chuck pops the cassette tape back in and mouths the words to "Long Time" while he drives. I'm reminded of the way when you're young and frustrated or lovelorn and you drive around listening to music, it speaks to you directly, seems to be the answer. My brother Ralph spent hours learning the opening riff of this song on an electric guitar. That year he grew his hair long, outraging my father with every inch it went past his collar. He told Dad he didn't have time to work on cars and his plans for college were out.

"Do you see these hands? See them!" my Dad used to say to both of us, holding up his battered, oil-stained hands: his way of saying that working on engines professionally would be a fate worse than death, that the cumulative struggles and ultimate redemption of his family line—his father the butcher and his father's father the dirt farmer—now depended on us. When I won a National Merit Finalist scholarship to college, my parents cried and looked to the heavens like lottery winners.

I'll never forget passing my brother's room one afternoon. My father was standing in there, holding an album cover—David Bowie's *The Rise and Fall of Ziggy*

Stardust and the Spiders from Mars. I stopped when it occurred to me how out of place he seemed. A black light picked up bits of grime sparkling on the back of his neck. He stared at the foldout art, holding it at arm's length. Then he ripped the cover in half with one swift motion. He saw the art as a poison against decent values. I was working on my Junior Achievement project that night when Ralph came downstairs with the torn cover, befuddled. Dad told him he was lucky everything in his room hadn't been ripped apart, that he knew all the things Ralph had been up to and it would have to *stop.*

Ralph stared at my father, quaking with anger. Then he looked at me and said, "Let's go, Bill." After he said it a second time, I went.

"Stay out!" my Dad yelled from the front door at Ralph, maybe me too. We got into Ralph's Toyota truck and he screeched off, cursing and slapping the steering wheel.

"Well?" he demanded of me.

"Well what?"

"Whose side are you on?"

"I'm on your side."

Lighting a cigarette, he didn't seem to hear me. With no moon, the headlights cut into a deep blackness. I flicked the radio dial around to whatever came in clear. At one point he sped up and said, "We can make Texas by morning," while flicking a butt out of the window.

"We can't go to Texas!" I said.

He pushed the gas pedal to the floor, the doors

shaking at 100 mph.

"Jesus, slow down!" I yelled.

That's when I started crying. Ralph looked over at me, then punched me in the shoulder. "Ease up, little brother." That made me mad.

We got back late that night. Ralph was in and out of the house, sleeping at friend's houses. On his eighteenth birthday he retrieved his clothes, left a long letter to my parents, gave me his record collection and a poem he'd written titled 'Standing on the Precipice.'

"Wait, you can't just leave," was all I could think to say.

"I can't?" He waved as he drove away.

We got postcards from Oregon and Alaska.

Ralph never made it to college. He started a company that builds log homes and makes great money. He built his own house, this fantastic hunting lodge, and works on most of his job sites. He wears flannel shirts, wielding an axe like the Brawny paper towel man.

I roll down my window and lean my head into the gust.

"You do your own work on this car?" I ask Chuck.

"Always have, always will. I know this car better than I know my own wretched self."

"How many miles you got?"

"Two hundred twenty thousand. And I've never had an accident."

Chuck is working the Charger. We're hitting all the green lights and he's passing what little traffic is on the street, snarling past them. A stoplight catches us. People in a Lexus stare.

We come to a green light intersection and Chuck begins a left turn. A van tries to run the light and roars at us from the left, aimed at the driver side back tire. I brace for catastrophe as Chuck yanks the wheel hard. The van breaks and fishtails, the two cars spinning around and toward each other like a skating pair meeting at center ice. The sides of the cars crunch together. The rat box flies between the seats, hits the dash and lands sideways on my lap. As I gather my wits from the impact, I'm staring through the slats at a hairy tail.

"Son of a bitch," Chuck says, his mouth wide open. He points at the box, "Don't let him bite you," and steps out of the car.

I right the box and place it on the back seat.

A large man with a beer gut argues with Chuck in front of the car. The man points at the Charger and shouts. Chuck braces himself, rears back with a tightly coiled arm and punches the man in the face. Beer Gut charges Chuck, grabs him and gets him in a head lock and pounds the top of Chuck's head. Wailing and grunting. Chuck is yelling what sounds like *Hell! Hell!* No, he's yelling *Bill! Bill!*

So I am out of the car and dizzy on my feet. I grab Beer Gut around the neck. A thick arm springs back and boxes my nose. Bodies fall on top of me. A warm trickle of blood seeps into my mouth. Shouting and door slamming. Two policemen untangle Hank and Beer

Gut, handcuffs flash. Another one snaps my arms behind me, a knee in my back. I'm still playing the accident over in my mind in slow motion.

As the cops talk to Beer Gut by one patrol car, Chuck and I stand near another, shackled, two winded and dangerous men at the side of an intersection. I'm thinking it would be a stretch to arrest us because all Chuck did was... *to start the fight.*

"Now remember," I say to Chuck, "he threw the first punch."

"I think I hit him first."

"Listen. Very important. *He* threw the first punch."

"Oh, yeah. Gotcha."

A cop with a crew cut walks over to us, hands propped on his gun belt. "So what happened here?"

We say in unison: "He threw the first punch, officer."

They put Beer Gut in the back of a patrol car. He's got an outstanding criminal warrant. Chuck was duking it out with a felon. We're uncuffed and told we're free to go. Every tension drains out of me in a sudden rush. I'm forty pounds lighter. Remember swimming the length of the pool underwater, then coming up for a breath?

Chuck takes a last look at the scraped, rumpled side of the car and gets back in. He smiles ear to ear, his face still reddened from punches. "You tricky devil. He started it!"

I laugh at Chuck's goofy, splotchy face. Our adrenaline is still going, mixing with everything else in our system and we're soaring on the wings of personal liberty. Chuck retells the fight blow by blow.

I notice blood stains on the ill-fated silk jacket. An elbow is ripped and frayed. I wipe dried blood off my lip with a lapel and toss the jacket onto the back seat. A vision comes: me suited up in Kendo gear, ignoring every thousand-year rule and savagely teeing off on Jerry like I'm swinging for the fences with a Louisville Slugger. Also, I'll buy that David Bowie album and mail it to Ralph. He'll laugh. Maybe I could get behind the wheel of the Charger. I'll ask Chuck.

I point at the dash clock. "Oh boy, the time. Somebody is gonna be unhappy."

"Unhappy?" Chuck says. "An understatement. Hey, before we go back, let's see if my python will eat this rat."

"What the hell."

He spins the steering wheel and floors it, then turns up the stereo. Chuck is wiping his forehead, mumbling something to me. We buzz through a turn, my stomach swaying. I get a nasty chill. What if Chuck and I had been busted for assault? I'd be sitting in lockup considering my fresh criminal record. I pull my seat belt across my lap, snap it in, and tighten the strap. Or what if that Cro-Magnon had slit my throat? Would the excitement have been worth it? Beating up Jerry seems rather extreme. A grudge could be started. No sense throwing away a lucrative situation.

My mind flashes back to that place behind the aging subdivision, to that shitty mixed-use neighborhood and a razor wire and hound dog protected inner sanctum. I realize that place, with its calloused hands and greasy independence, shines like a veritable heaven. Suddenly, it burns brightly in me—a Hank's place in my mind.

Chuck accelerates up a highway ramp, singing, the engine roaring. Thailand is a lush, lush place. Swooping in from the Gulf of Siam you see the most robust emerald imaginable. The Charger merges, howling past other cars. I grip the door, wide-eyed, my outstretched foot hovering over an imaginary brake.

SAUNTER

I ce: the object of his desire. Summer humidity was in full blast. Jim had concluded a long and satisfying yoga session. Every limb was spry with a relaxed vigor. His being centered, dots of sweat pooled among the hair follicles on his arms, a stippled wave across his forehead. A thirst came to him—from exertion and the hot climate of his second floor apartment. His air was not conditioned. He did not require this. Roxanne, the woman who owned the Victorian house and occupied the first floor, did not provide it. He may have purchased a window unit and paid an electric bill surcharge, but again, he did not require this.

Most Americans associated heat with oppression and misery. And true, a patience was required to sleep under warm sheets or with a sticky film on one's chest. However, the rigor of summer had a certain restorative, cleansing power as well. This was overlooked. For the entire history of man, with the exception of the last fifty years, summer had been a time of heat, of perspiration. But it wasn't good enough, and people were now doing absurd things like plugging phone lines into their computers to talk to other computers.

He opened his freezer and looked into the icebox, smelling stale plastic air. He could have had chilled vegetable juice, or placed water within the refrigerator and waited, yet his preference for ice cubes remained. The local market four blocks away had a commercial ice maker on the sidewalk. With a plastic cup in hand, he opened the door to his apartment, prepared to descend the outside metal steps. On the landing he froze—an instinctive pause—not knowing why. A brief senility. Jim looked down. He had been doing his yogic distortions with a bare minimum of clothing, both to stay cool and to allow unencumbered movement. Bleach white underwear, nothing else. What are known as briefs. He didn't know the brand, but one identical in design and appearance he knew to be made by one Calvin Klein. They fit snugly while allowing full movement, a cotton skin. Sitting on the floor in the lotus position, his head shaved, barefoot, briefs hugging his hips—he thought of a loin-clothed Gandhi on a sandy floor.

From the backyard a breeze licked at his legs. Oh, the disappointment. Feeling so centered and right, so ready for liquid nourishment, his feet bursting, eager to stroll, yet he'd hit societal piano wire. More clothing would have to be added. The prospect of a shirt suffocating his skin, soaking up droplets that would otherwise evaporate, or pants wrapping around his limbs—flapping and chafing like tarpaulin tent flaps— sank him to untold depths. A questioning began. He was in no danger of violating decency laws. Why his hesitancy? He was bound by a prickly vine of unwritten rules: fashion, a tacit means of control.

Birds chirped in a trellis, a squirrel skittered across the backyard. Blades of grass stretched to a sublime cerulean sky. And why not? He found himself gliding down the stairs, sucked along.

As a child growing up in a subdivision, at a certain point he stopped seeing the identical brick ranch houses, backyard trampolines, abandoned Big Wheels, carports and moldering bags of barbeque charcoal. It all smeared in his vision by age eleven—with the exception of *The Twilight Zone*. Sitting exactly two feet in front of his family's color floor unit television Jim watched with intensity: lips parted, teeth pressed together as Rod Serling—clearly a man of worldly knowledge, of gravitas—spun tales of book-loving men given isolation and all eternity to read, yet without functioning eyeglasses; of neighbors driven to violence by unfounded suspicion; of people trapped in existential rooms with strangers, unaware of a cruel fate that awaited them, or that had trapped them all ready. His younger sisters stood at a distance from him and the television, unsure if they should approach.

His *aha* moment: the people in the subdivision were the same people bedeviled in the half hour stories. He lived in the Zone. And the Zone was all he could see standing on his two feet, or hope to see, from the cargo area of a station wagon. And to spend your life in the Zone, unaware, engaged in pointless pursuits as a disturbing fate circled silently over your head, seemed a disappointing destiny.

It was not until he stumbled upon actor David Carradine in reruns of the television series *Kung Fu* that he sensed, with brimming excitement, there was something else. There was another way, but it was unclear how that worked.

It was a matter of accessing it.

Then came a paperback copy of Isaac Asimov's *Foundation Trilogy*, which, to his father's great chagrin, he chose to read during his family's weekly visit to the Pentecostal church. His father, a potential shouter on any given day, even when Jim brought home straight A report cards, ripped book two of the *Trilogy* and threw the halves at his feet. Church was a high energy place with its own band, and a sweaty man dressed in a white suit who gave rambling, possessed sermons. As a twelve-year-old, Jim had been moved by wild shouts from parishioners in surrounding pews to briefly stand up in his brown polyester suit and clip-on tie. But post *Trilogy*, he reflexively distrusted the pastor and tuned him out. Post divorce of his parents at age sixteen, he discovered *The Bhagavad-Gita* and memorized passages in his room.

His tattoo of an Egyptian hieroglyph on his left bicep prompted his eviction from his father's house. Living with mom, without funds to attend college, he took a job shelving goods in a supermarket. In the early nineties, he stood before a roaring ten-foot speaker stack at an Alice in Chains concert. The hairs on his neck twitched and his chest palpated like a drum kit. During the song "Man in a Box" he received a major transmission: *Go forth!* His earliest travels were to Mexico and Central America. I mean, what was living but moving from one place to another? He earned money as he needed it, then learned to live without money. After all, every restaurant threw away perfectly good food on a daily basis. The trick was to find the better establishments.

This was how things worked in the Zone.

But was he still in the Zone? At times, such as when deep in a jungle or under the stars of the desert, he felt on the verge of escaping. Until he dragged himself into town to get more food, and there they all were.

He had been on the road a long time. He was tight on funds, his belt one notch tighter than he was accustomed. A disharmony had interrupted his chakra channel. His cellular energies were tweaking, his kundalini whipsawed between stimulation and intransigence. These weren't impediments, they were signs. Plus, it was the year before the new millennium. So it was time to root, which is occasionally necessary when finding what you seek. He sensed it was within grasp.

An ad for the room hung at the local A & P. He knocked at the listed house and a slender woman in faded jeans, with scattered, shoulder length hair opened the door. Roxanne looked him over through her locked storm door. She adjusted her brown glasses. His pack on one shoulder and a beard down to his chest. He smiled and bowed slightly, his hands palm to palm at his chin. She started to shake her head *No*, then rethought it and opened the door, keeping her eyes carefully on him.

"Does this window face east?" he asked her in the upstairs apartment.

She pulled her eyebrows low, thinking. "Southeast, I believe." Divine streaks of gray ran through her dark hair. Careful lines distinguished her green eyes. He took her in, as he might a blooming tree or a sunset over a plateau.

He glanced at the simple bed and the kitchenette, then sat on the floor beneath a window, his spine perfectly erect, his chin even with the sill. Roxanne watched him, blinking. "This will do just fine," he said.

"I have extra furniture in the garage. A couch, some chairs."

"I don't need them."

She shook her head in disbelief, then shrugged.

He kept to himself the first month, ghostly rushes of running water the only upstairs sounds. He emerged from his apartment barefoot one morning, head and face shaved, in white cotton pants and T-shirt. From the driveway she did a double take, then studied him carefully. He waved politely. She chuckled to herself, then waved back. A tiny wave of excitement went through him, which he quickly throttled.

He had a long history of misreading feminine cues.

It was so hard to read the thoughts of other human beings. In sixth grade, his mind whirring like a pinball machine after an algebra lecture, he sat by Josie Quillam during lunch and started talking excitedly to her about fractals. In class she had taken copious notes, he'd noticed, and he assumed she was equally enthusiastic. But Josie just stared at him, mute and big-eyed, with what seemed like confusion or fright, or both. He endured the rest of lunch in silence, unable to risk further interaction.

He got a job shelving books at the library. He knocked on Roxanne's front door one Saturday holding old hardback books. When she opened the door he said, "These are replaced editions. Rilke, the poet. A modern genius, yes?"

A bemused smile crept across her face. "I don't know him."

He observed her standing in the doorway, then said, "The library is giving them away." He held the books up higher for her inspection.

She opened the door wide and motioned him in. He stepped in, his eyes focused on the floor. She sat on her beige velour sectional couch. With an expression of sleepy awe, he sat on the other end. She tilted her head to see the bottoms of his feet, thick with calluses.

"Does it hurt to walk around like that?" she asked matter-of-factly.

He complicated the question briefly, thinking of 'hurt' in broad philosophical terms, as in universal suffering, then decided to say, "It's what feet were made to do."

He opened a tattered edition of Jack London's *White Fang* and read a passage about wolves circling in a whirling snowstorm. She swiveled her head slowly, following the narrative. He closed the book and looked at her with docile eyes.

"Have you read this?" he asked expectantly.

She shook her head.

"Then you should have it." He presented the book with both hands.

"Thank you." She glanced at it briefly, then put it aside.

Several moments passed as they looked at each other. She squirmed, picking at the fringe of a pillow. "I used to write poetry," she said.

He nodded in comprehension. "I would like to read some."

He climbed the outside metal stairs to his room with a stack of typed pages. He locked the door and lit a candle and read sitting on the floor. Pausing after every line, he let the words settle in. He read a long poem titled, *When Will The Robins Return?* It was repetitive, though sincere. She'd put work into the poems. She had a depth. Late that night he blew out the candle.

I have seen into her soul, he said to himself.

Standing on his metal balcony, he watched her emerge from her car in the driveway. "I read them all," he shouted. He softly clapped his hands and did a partial bow. She put a hand to her eyebrows and smiled, squinting up at him.

Weeks later, Roxanne tapped at his door. "I'm very sorry to intrude." Her hands shook, eyes aflame, her voice a weird alto. "Moxy… my dog, has been run over." She put a hand on her chest. "I can't possibly do it myself."

He went out to the street and found a fluffy carcass spotted with damp red stains. He ran his hand under its belly and placed it in a plastic trash bag. He remembered the wild rabbit he'd trapped and eaten in South Dakota, its charred scent.

Sitting on the couch, she nestled a cordless phone back into its cradle. "Animal control will come pick her up." She wiped a tear from her eye. "You must think me quite insane."

"Of course not." He sat beside her. He found himself falling into her sadness, into rage at the world's unfairness—a faulty notion.

"I had her over nine years." Roxanne sobbed into her hands. He watched her rounded back quiver. He slid toward her and said, "I'm sorry." He put his arm at the top of the cushion where she sat—hoping it was the right thing to do and that he was doing it correctly. She turned and folded into him. Her eyes wet his shoulder.

He recalled the last time he'd been this close to a woman, years ago in Costa Rica. An English woman wearing a PJ Harvey t-shirt had consumed a mushroom milkshake and started raving on the beach in distress. He'd eaten one himself days before. He calmed her, speaking in low, gentle tones. They stayed up most of the moonlit night, sitting cross-legged and facing each other on moist black sand, chatting about the universe and religion and science and pointing out stars. The most stimulating conversation he'd ever had with another human. The next day he ran into her at breakfast. At first, she barely recognized him. Then she laughed, thanked him for saving her and said, "I was so fucking high." She spent her remaining days with her friends. Their relationship was a bright comet that had streaked across the sky, leaving a trail of fading dust.

With the light outside dimming, Roxanne fell asleep. His arm hovering over her went numb. In darkness, he listened to her breathing. When he couldn't tolerate the spiky pain of his arm any longer, he lowered it to her shoulder. The skin of her upper arm tingled underneath his hand. He'd forgotten the warmth and semi-slick texture of skin not your own.

Roxanne invited him to dinner one evening, on her forty-second birthday, exactly one month away from his thirty-second. The day after the winter solstice. After fasting and a sleepless night of intensive meditation, he found it hard to keep his eyes open. He knocked at her door wearing jeans and a clean white T-shirt. She greeted him with a small hug, unusual in itself. Then the fragrance: a sweet, rich lilac and violet cocktail. He had never been aware of her having an odor. He stayed close to her a moment, fixating, finding an intensity in the olfactory experience, mixed with an early memory involving a grammar schoolteacher. He noticed her smiling at him. This was puzzling.

Sitting in a straight back chair felt peculiar, as though the seat might collapse. A circular pattern in the tablecloth mesmerized him. He corralled peas on one side of his plate, set a somber lump of mashed potatoes next to them and laid out a piece of haddock, centering it. He chewed some peas, staring at his fork.

"Is something wrong?" she asked.

"On the contrary. Everything is fine." The home cooked meal awakened his taste buds. Food could be a joy, though sustenance was reward enough.

She peered at the side of his shaved head, at the scars over his ear. "What happened there?" Then she said, "Oh my God. I don't mean to pry."

"It's okay. I was in a soap box derby race when I was a kid. A wheel came off and the car flipped. My head scraped the pavement." He left out the part about the concussion, and vomiting for days.

A look of horror on her face. "They should make those things safer."

"I made it myself."

"Did your Dad help?"

He winced to think of his father. "I didn't want his help," he said blankly.

She blinked, taking in this information.

She spoke of a brother in a distant city. He had suffered a career setback after his company restructured. He and Roxanne were fraternal twins. She stopped talking and looked at him and he realized he needed to say something, anything, since there was a void in the conversation. So he asked, "Does he look like you?"

"We used to. I don't think we do anymore. You be the judge." She pulled a photo album out of a drawer. In a high school photo, her brother wore a tie and had round gold framed glasses, his hair a careful wave.

"I see a resemblance." Both their eyes conveyed a trusting amazement.

"Do you have any siblings?" she asked gingerly.

"Two younger sisters. One is married." He'd heard this after calling his mother, years back. He wasn't sure what cities they lived in now. Eight months ago, he thought he'd seen his youngest sister on a Vancouver sidewalk. She'd been the one, years before, to say there was concern about him.

"I have tickets to the symphony this month," Roxanne said brightly. "They're doing Mahler. Let me know if you'd like to go."

Music played by an orchestra appealed to him suddenly, the string section, the fine acoustics, accompanying Roxanne, until he saw the look of expectation on her face. *What am I doing?* he thought. What scenario am I being drawn into? Everyone at the symphony would be dressed like bourgeois robber barons, smoking cancerous devices in the lobby. It was so pathetically Zone. He'd been distracted by enough frivolity.

He thanked her for the meal, held her hand briefly between his, then left.

On that day, when birds chirped in a trellis and a squirrel skittered across the backyard, he stood on the metal stairs. Wearing only snug white briefs around his hips and buttocks, his limbs clear and buoyant, liberated. And why not? He glided down the stairs. At the bottom gravel tweaked his toes and the smooth wide stones leading to the garden pressed against his arches. He heard the sound of a spade striking earth. He peered over an ivy-covered brick wall, leaves scratching his chest and neck.

"So you've come down to help weed," Roxanne said, adjusting her gloves.

"I'm on a mission." By his face he held a plastic cup, soon to be filled with ice cubes.

"One day I'll find you wilted up there."

"Worry is never necessary."

"You seem chipper today." She smiled, one of her high cheek bones smudged with something, maybe manure. *Chipper*, that peculiarly American word. She brightened: "Cooked way too much lasagna. Could you drop in to help me finish it?"

"Certainly. Waste must be avoided."

"You could use a big meal. Tomorrow night?"

"Sure."

She smiled and returned her attention to the dirt.

He followed the garden wall to the side of the house, the driveway opening to the street. So far so good. On the sidewalk, the grandeur, the daring of his jaunt took hold, cement scratching the balls of his feet.

The trees were weighed full with lush boughs. Somewhere children splashed in pools, somewhere watermelon was being eaten, the earth turned slowly on its tilt. He slowed his pace to savor it all. *Saunter.* Henry David Thoreau's glorious word. He sensed this walk had potential. He recalled walking the southern coast of Nicaragua, the trails of the Sierra Nevada mountains. Why had he never done this before?

A dog walker passed him, an older gentleman who snorted and yanked his retriever away, both of them scurrying off. Brief self-consciousness welled, and then it passed. A couple tapped numbers into an ATM at the corner. A car honked somewhere as he crossed a street. Solitary drivers with placid expressions drifted past.

In front of the convenience store, he scooped a heaping load of ice, the crystals gleaming like wet diamonds. He crunched a mouthful, his tongue growing frigid. Inside, his friend Roger, sporting a turban and a Pittsburgh Steelers jersey, was behind the counter. Roger chortled, "My friend, today you have become a sadhu!"

"Indeed. Ha."

Paying at the counter, a twentyish woman nursing a Big Gulp looked him up and down.

"Are your earthly possessions in the scrap heap?" Roger asked.

"Far better if they were." He toasted Roger with the cup. He picked up a package of beef jerky rolls and strolled down an aisle. A man wearing brown slacks and a button up shirt pulled a Yoo-Hoo out of the refrigerator wall. He dropped his gaze as Jim neared, his mouth and jaw tightening visibly in displeasure. Mean-while, a stocky, scruffy man—a roofer, if the black smears on his T-shirt were to be believed—stood further down the aisle, wearing thin synthetic shorts: an amount of fabric barely more than Jim's, yet this man wasn't on Brown Slacks' radar, and never would be. Jim shook his head at the irrationality and inconsistency of it.

He selected whole grain sandwich bread and stood in line at the counter.

"Do you miss the rainy season?" he asked Roger. Roger had been in the states only a few years. The last member of his family to trickle through from India.

"What normal person would miss torrential downpours day and night?"

"Yes, but the relief when they come."

"True. Now I'm sentimental."

He put the jerky and bread next to the register. Jim realized his predicament with paying at the same time Roger said. "Where have you put your billfold, Mr. World Citizen?" Jim smiled awkwardly. They both chuckled, until Roger said: "I will sponsor you in your quest."

"Many thanks." Jim made prayer hands.

"Bring it next time."

Outside the air had turned edgy. Hard overhead sun rays spiked the ground. Sitting traffic cooked up billows of carbon monoxide. Scrunched faces behind mirrored eye wear and tinted windshields. Ice in hand, he contemplated turning home, but his mission was in-complete. Sometimes, early in meditation, bricks are flung about in one's consciousness—distractions, pitfalls, some nasty prevalent thought, a gnat to be shirked or subdued. One can never give up then. To do so would invite the same bird to light on your shoulder the next time and the next, growing as a devouring chimera. One persevered until breaking through. On the same path of sidewalk, he headed downtown, holding his goods with the arm opposite from the street.

A bus drove away from a stop, thundering, grating his ear drums. An acorn pinched the bottom of his heel. He passed a long provincial lawn. Utility poles slick with black tar ticked ahead over a hill. A breeze licked his limbs and he felt energized, simplified, like a prophet of old. Maybe, he thought, the way to defeat the Zone was to defy its conventions. Had he found a soft spot?

A car coming toward him on his side of the street slowed—Roxanne's Volvo. He leaned down to look in the open window and offered, "Hello."

Her lips moved without sound coming out. Leaning over the passenger seat, her eyes took him in then darted up and down the street.

"What happened?" Roxanne asked.

"Nothing happened."

"Let me give you a ride, Jim," she said, nodding her head vigorously.

"That's okay. Just stretching my legs."

Her eyebrows were nearly vertical with concern.

"Are you sure?"

"Positive."

She clamped her lips together and drove on, not looking back. He watched the car disappear, thinking that she seemed in a hurry to get somewhere. His eyes lifted to the cloudless blue sky, the perfection of it suddenly overwhelming. He exhaled and tilted his head back. He wished he could strip off the briefs.

At an intersection he paused for a crossing signal. Chaotic guitar music blared suddenly. Voices from a black Jeep containing young, smooth faces. A teenage male leaned out the door, waving a shirt. "You forgot your pants, stupid idiot!" Heads and hair tossed under the roll bar, piercings flashing. Whooping sounds. Jim walked on, the gargantuan inky tires of the jeep jerking beside him. Screeching and pointing. "Hey, man! Hey!"

He had thoroughly considered the circumstances that rendered him thus. All quite natural, quite reasonable. They stood on their own weight. In this spirit, he turned his head and sent compassionate vibes their way. A young woman crouching in the back flung a soda can that sailed past him and tinged against the sidewalk. "Motherfucker!" The vehicle sprung off, a Medusa of pale arms and swaying torsos. He stood still to moderate his heartbeat, adopting the half-smile of the Buddha.

He went on with renewed vigor. Down a bare hill tall buildings opened up in the distance. Perspiration dribbled over his cheeks. He passed parking lots and crumbling knee-high brick abutments. He skipped over bits of broken glass, treading nimbly.

Nearing a set of low-rises, a pounding jangly roar came from the other side of a hill. The Jeep packed with teenagers blasted along.

He grabbed an oil can in his path, a heavy ruster, and identified two more in easy reach. They drove past him, shrieking and hooting. He tested the heft of the can, waiting for the vehicle to turn around, for the confrontation. It never happened, but he flung the can anyway, almost losing his footing. As it banged on the distant sidewalk he felt something loosen from his mind and drain into the ether.

He realized he had always been hauling something around: caring about what they thought. Even in the deepest forest or most deserted wasteland, even in perfect stillness when praying to the universe. Ever since lunch time with Josie Quillam, he'd carried around his neck the negative judgement of their conventions—the shutters of a brick ranch could be painted black or dark green, but yellow and tangerine were not to be considered and might earn a knock at your door from enraged neighbors. Always the dualism of right and wrong.

His blood pressure spiked and he lunged for the second can, a low roar escaping from him. With his full might he smashed it against a boarded storefront. He dropped into a squat, holding his head between his hands. Breathing through clenched teeth, he waited for his pulse to moderate.

What he remembered about the rest of that miraculous day was losing track of his individual footfalls, like he was coasting on cloud cover. Faces flashed around him, but he heard nothing. He caught hold of his reflection in a mirrored skyscraper wall—a glow, a corona surrounding his limbs, bleaching out the suit and leather shoe crowd who seemed to be suspended in plasma around him. *I'm free*, he thought, and how weird that the Zone could just fade out like a ghost passing through a wall.

Deep in the pit of evening, he cooled his toes in a brook beside a dirt road, the glow of the city faded, heavy stars overhead. He shivered, overcome by what had transpired.

He got back in time for dinner the next day. He toweled off, put on fresh briefs and went down to Roxanne's front door. Since she'd seen him, she wouldn't need prepping about his experience. He decided to offer it as conversation. He had an expansive grin as she looked out the inlay glass.

She opened the door, stepped into the doorway and crossed her arms. He wondered how he was supposed to get in with her standing there.

"Let me tell you about yesterday," he began.

"Looks like yesterday never ended."

"Perhaps, it has not." His eyes gleamed. She'd suddenly become more perceptive. He thought maybe they had neared the same plane.

"This is what you do with my invitation?"

Confused, he leaned forward two inches. Was this teasing? "I am here."

"So you are." She left the door open and he followed her inside. In the dining room, he realized: she was offended by his clothing. But here he stood, and she, of all people, might understand. So he would try again.

He nibbled at cornbread, trying to engage Roxanne's gaze from the opposite side of the table. She ate with distraction, her eyes fixed on her plate.

He probed a few times about his experience, saying "Remember, when you ran through sprinklers as a child?" and, "Have you ever thought you had seen another side?" She gave vague responses and listened guardedly, her careful and beautiful self, excusing herself several times to check the progress of a dessert. Explanations were for those seeking glory or exercising pride.

He stopped talking and worked his fork with humility. Quietly musing, he lapsed into the previous day. Into the pleasant buzz behind his temples, the playful shadows of clouds passing across his path. Beneath his feet, the planet wobbled in its orbit. Like a subatomic particle in flight, he sped along with a flawless continuity of motion. He understood so many things yet had no need to understand.

Roxanne cleared the dishes with pale, veined hands. He clicked on the radio in her parlor to some jazz, watching her kitchen profile. The sound of sax and trumpet in merry tandem, backed by clever drum work. It opened a primitive channel—the joy of music—and his fondness for her quaked forth, like an earthworm wriggling on pavement after a hard rain.

Finding a buoyancy in his knees, he snagged her on a return trip to the dining room. He snaked his arm around to the small of her back, holding her opposite hand high, pulling her close enough to smell her shampoo. His elastic waist band rubbed against her jeans. They glided together a moment—was it dancing? She looked over his shoulder, her chin high. Then a stiffness glaciated her body, until he could only do a tepid waltz around her.

At last she met his gaze, her eyes piercing and wide with some welling from inside her, which he feared to be revulsion. The tip of her tongue floated inside her mouth.

Three months later, in Tulsa, two sheriff's deputies wearing squawking radios beat him with batons. They found his explanation for his appearance to be insolent. That night in a shelter, he noted with clinical detachment the splotchy contusions and lumps along his arms and legs. They throbbed like alternating lights. A volunteer worker, who'd had to persist in her offer of treatment, swabbed encrusted blood off his eyebrow with a sterile solution.

The gesture brought Roxanne to mind, her face still fresh in his memory. He remembered his last dance. Her waist had been warm under his hand. Then, suddenly, in unison, they stepped away from each other, as if each had been startled by a loud noise. Arms at their sides, they stared in charged silence. He quietly left and packed his things that night, leaving behind a note that said: *Thank you so much for all.*

As he had turned to leave, her eyebrows were high, which he had thought signified rage. But on second thought, it might have meant disappointment. Her expression almost seemed… forlorn? Her fingers had flared out, then they fluttered next to her hips, as if they were suddenly nervous or were seeking to embrace something else. He remembered her poised tongue, and it occurred to him she was about to say something important. He regretted not having pressed her to say it. And wasn't this the problem with other humans, always the confusion about what was rolling around in the other person's skull.

He realized there was a way to resolve the mystery about what she had wanted to say. He could just ask her.

ABOUT THE AUTHOR

Robb Skidmore's short stories have appeared in many reviews and publications. He is the author of a novella, *The Surfer,* and a novel, *The Pursuit of Cool,* a coming-of-age story set in the 1980s. He currently lives in Southern California.

If you wish to be alerted to new book releases, please subscribe to his website at www.robbskidmore.com.